The
Disappeared

Gloria Whelan

DIAL BOOKS

DIAL BOOKS • A member of Penguin Group (USA) Inc. • Published by The Penguin Group • Penguin Group (USA) Inc., 375 Hudson Street, New York, NY 10014, U.S.A. • Penguin Group (Canada), 90 Eglinton Avenue East, Suite 700, Toronto, Ontario, Canada M4P 2Y3 (a division of Pearson Penguin Canada Inc.) Penguin Books Ltd, 80 Strand, London WC2R 0RL, England • Penguin Ireland, 25 St. Stephen's Green, Dublin 2, Ireland (a division of Penguin Books Ltd) • Penguin Group (Australia), 250 Camberwell Road, Camberwell, Victoria 3124, Australia (a division of Pearson Australia Group Pty Ltd) • Penguin Books India Pvt Ltd, 11 Community Centre, Panchsheel Park, New Delhi - 110 017, India • Penguin Group (NZ), 67 Apollo Drive, Rosedale, North Shore 0632, New Zealand (a division of Pearson New Zealand Ltd) • Penguin Books (South Africa) (Pty) Ltd, 24 Sturdee Avenue, Rosebank, Johannesburg 2196, South Africa • Penguin Books Ltd, Registered Offices: 80 Strand, London WC2R 0RL, England

The publisher does not have any control over and does not assume any responsibility for author or third-party websites or their content.

Designed by Peonia Vázquez-D'Amico
Text set in Granjon
Printed in the U.S.A.

10 9 8 7 6 5 4 3 2 1

Library of Congress Cataloging-in-Publication Data
Whelan, Gloria.
The Disappeared / Gloria Whelan.
p. cm.
Summary: Teenaged Silvia tries to save her brother, Eduardo, after he is captured by the military government in 1970s Argentina.
Includes bibliographical references.
ISBN 978-0-8037-3275-9
1. Argentina—History—Dirty War, 1976–1983—Juvenile fiction. [1. Argentina—History—Dirty War, 1976–1983—Fiction. 2. Disappeared persons—Fiction. 3. Brothers and sisters—Fiction.] I. Title.
PZ7.W5718Di 2008
[Fic]—dc22
2007043750

For
Joyce Carol Oates

ACKNOWLEDGMENTS

I would like to express my gratitude to Alisha Niehaus and Shelley Diaz, who made this journey with me, and to Salvador, who all these years has shared his love and knowledge of Argentina.

Buenos Aires
1977

Silvia

EDUARDO, it happened hours ago but I relive it again and again. All the lights in our neighborhood went out. I thought nothing of it, for I had read that the workers in the electric plants were staging blackouts because of a wage cut. You, dear brother, understood at once. You had heard stories from the others. The whole neighborhood was darkened so no one could see which house the military police broke into.

It was ours.

We were all together. Father had just returned from a late night at the hospital and was telling us of an interesting patient. "This man is so rigid and stiff, he can no longer sit or walk, a tragic but fascinating case. I'm writing it up for the journal." Mother was listening carefully. Perhaps she was wondering how she could use the strange disease in a poem. Her poems are quilts of the pieces of our lives turned every which way so that we seem to be both ourselves and people we do not know. I sat next to you on the couch, my legs curled cozily under me, relieved that for once we were all together with no arguments.

At the first pounding your red setter, Dichoso, barked wildly and threw himself at the door. Father gathered us around him. They forced the door open, giving Dichoso a brutal kick. Men wearing army uniforms and masks stormed into the house, making it their own. They placed a hood over your face, handcuffed you, and carried you away—pushing aside Father as he pleaded to go in your place. Mother grasped my hand so tightly I winced. She held on to me as she wanted to hold on to you, Eduardo, and could not.

More masked men swarmed over the house, turning everything upside down. They emptied your room, carrying away your beloved books. One of the soldiers purposely brushed against me, leering. Then they were gone. The house had never felt so empty.

Dear Eduardo, dear brother, how is it that you and I argued so much? That is the terrible, wonderful thing about how much we love each other; everything matters and everything can hurt. I can't send these letters to you, but if I write them in my heart I know that wherever they have taken you, you will hear them.

Our country is at war with itself. Argentina has become a battlefield, a country of death and of mourners. Just as we are brother and sister, Eduardo, and our quarrels tear at our hearts, so our people fight one another to the death. It is the cruelest kind of war.

Do you remember how happy we once were, how you and I shared the city? We were *porteños,* people of the port. The parks, decorated with their pink and purple bougainvillea blossoms, were our play yard. Do you remember our first visit to the zoo? I was no larger than the penguins. We fell in love with the white tiger, a pale ghost of an animal. When the lions roared we laughed. Nothing frightened us, for danger was safely caged. That was how we looked at the world then, believing nothing evil could reach us.

Mother took us to the Teatro Colón to see the operas. We saw misery and murder on the stage all dressed up in fine costumes, but when the curtain came down, the misery and murder disappeared. We went happily home whistling the tunes. On Sundays we would walk with our parents among the trees and tombstones of Recoleta. It was not so much a cemetery as a park. As we walked along the narrow avenues we were never frightened, for the tomb's great marble angels watched over us.

We went with Father to the *planetario* and looked up at the stars, the Southern Cross and the false cross. Father pointed to the constellation of the Phoenix. "The Phoenix," he said, "was a bird of the greatest possible beauty. Every five hundred years the bird was consumed by the burning rays of the sun, only to rise once again. The magnificent bird could not be destroyed. That is our country of Argentina," Father said. "There have been terrible times, and such times may come again, but Argentina will survive." Then the guerrillas came, and the generals after them, snatching away our childhood and destroying our home.

Your arguments with Father began the day the military police came to his hospital. It was a warm spring day. You and I were sitting with Mother on the terrace. After Mother complained about the neighbor's cat stalking our birds, you chased it out of our yard with a broom. I was reading an English spy story that had just been translated into Spanish.

On the table was a pitcher of iced tea and a bowl of strawberries. We all looked up, surprised at hearing Father's car pull into the garage in the middle of the day. He walked out onto the terrace and sank into a chair as if he had been walking for miles.

"What is it, Arturo?" Mother asked.

"They came to the hospital today," Father said.

"Who came?" you asked, Eduardo, but from your expression I knew you had already guessed. "The police?"

"Yes," Father said, "the police. They took away Jacobo Solanas, the doctor that heads up our psychiatric service."

"Why?" Mother asked, her voice incredulous. "I've met Jacobo at parties with you. There's not a political bone in his body."

"The generals have the idea that Solanas's patients have confided secrets to him—and secrets are dangerous. They're taking him in for questioning. They want to see if any of those secrets are a danger to the state. I know Solanas. He will not give away what his patients have told him in confidence. He will end up in prison."

You were furious, Eduardo, and demanded of Father, "What are you going to do about it?"

"I can do nothing. I'm a doctor and not a politician."

You asked, "Why don't you protest? How could you let them take Dr. Solanas away?"

"How would it help my patients if I were put in jail? And what would it mean for you and your mother and Silvia to have a father shut away in prison?"

You lashed out at Father. "Do you think I would care about that! The important thing is to fight, to fight against the generals who are taking away our freedom."

Mother said, "Think what you're saying, Eduardo. You would have your father throw himself into the lions' den."

Father said, "Eduardo, you're being an impetuous fool. I've taken an oath to heal the sick, and that's exactly what I will do. I will not be drawn into this political nightmare."

You would not be silenced. "I don't see how you can turn your back on Dr. Solanas. If you and the other medical faculty don't do something, who will speak out for him? I'll go to the hospital myself tomorrow! I can get some of my friends to demonstrate."

"You will do nothing of the kind. This is not a

time for heroics. In this country, all the heroes end up dead."

Mother fled to her study to write a poem. She puts all her fear and anger into her poems, but she no longer publishes them. Alma, the editor of her poetry magazine, has disappeared. Now Mother can only write her poems of protest on thick paper, each word cutting into the paper like a knife. She locks the dangerous poems away in her desk so that you can almost hear the imprisoned words screaming to be let out.

"What good will a poem do Dr. Solanas?" you demanded. "No one will see it. The generals are sure to close down any magazine that would dare to print it."

Father had the last word. "You will stay out of this matter, Eduardo. One ill-considered word can lock you away for a lifetime, or worse. Just do what I'll do. Keep very quiet."

I was terrified. Like everyone else I had heard stories of arrests and disappearances. Now it was happening in Father's own hospital. What if it happened to Father? I wasn't brave or brash like you, Eduardo. I believed if we were quiet and did nothing, we would all be safe. I decided to pretend the nightmares were not happening. I would be the little mouse and make myself small so the cat would not find me.

I made a different world for myself with my friends Rosa and Isabela. We three were inseparable, keeping close, and pretending there was nothing wrong, that the frightening tales told in whispers were all in people's imagination. After school we rode Palermo Viejo's bike paths. We window-shopped on Florida Street for jeans and shoes with heels so high, we could hardly walk on them. We went to the *heladerías* to munch on double chocolate cones sprinkled with *granizados* and then the next day, knowing how fattening the ice cream was, we would go to the Café Tortoni, eating nothing, only drinking black coffee. Afterwards we would weaken and end up with a *pancho* or an *empanada* from one of the *kioscos*. We put on our party dresses and had tea at the Alvear Palace Hotel, pretending we were sophisticated and elegant. We sneaked out of our houses to go to the discos and danced until it was light and time to get ready for our classes.

It was at a disco that I first met Norberto. He insisted on dancing every dance with me, and glared at any boy who tried to cut in. He was tall with slicked-back brown hair and cold blue eyes. He watched me in a way that made me want to close the top button of my blouse, but he was an excellent dancer. "Tell me the name of your favorite song," he said. "I'll get the band to play it."

"'He Will Break Your Heart,'" I said. I was just getting over Alfonso from school, but I didn't tell Norberto that. Norberto went over to the band leader and I saw him give the man a lot of money. They played the song and then he asked them to play Paul McCartney's song "And I Love Her."

"That's for you, beautiful," he said. I had never had a band play a song I wanted. It made me feel important, as if I could pick out anything in the world and Norberto would give it to me.

Isabela had been watching us. She took me aside and whispered, "That boy you are dancing with is Norberto López. He's the son of General López, the general who shut down the university paper and arrested the professors."

I couldn't believe her. Norberto just seemed like a boy interested in having a good time. "Are you sure?"

"Of course I'm sure. He's at the university with my brother. Norberto is always reminding people of how high up in the government his father is and how they have expensive cars and a vacation home in Tigre.

Everyone dislikes him but they're afraid to show it. They don't want him running to his father with their names. I would never dance with him, and neither should you."

"I had no idea. That's revolting. Watch me get rid of him." I made excuses not to dance with Norberto, careful not to make him angry. "I promised my girlfriends I'd go home with them," I told him. "It's been lots of fun."

"Give me your phone number," he demanded.

"My parents don't approve of phone calls from boys. They'd be upset. I promise I'll be back soon." I hurried out of the disco with Isabela and Rosa feeling as if I had escaped a dark woods where dangerous animals lurked.

I knew little of politics, but I had heard you, Eduardo, speak of General López's cruelty. He might even have been the one to arrest Professor Bustamante, who was your favorite. I remembered how upset you were when the professor disappeared, and I shivered with disgust to think I had been dancing with López's son. I was careful to say nothing to you about my evening with Norberto. After that I kept away from the disco.

I saw the way you disapproved of me, Eduardo.

"Silvia, how can you know so little of what's going on right under your own nose? How can you be so frivolous? Don't you care about what's happening to our country?"

I didn't want to think about the things that were happening. "Of course I care, but what good does it do to protest? The generals have all the power. It will only get us into trouble, Eduardo. Father is right. We should go on with our lives. Next year I'll be at the university and there will be nothing but work. I want to have fun my last free year."

I kept on trying to ignore what was happening. On Sundays after Mass, Rosa and Isabela and I would go to the Feria de San Telmo and browse the booths searching for vintage clothing, long velvet skirts, and little hats with veils. On sunny days we would go to the park and wander under the ancient magnolia trees, trees so old they had forgotten how to bloom.

All the while, Eduardo, I watched you draw away from our family and become more and more involved with meetings and demonstrations. I was frightened for you. Our country had a name for the prisoners who were arrested and never seen again. They were called *Los Desaparecidos*. The Disappeared. You would not let people forget those who had vanished. You marched with the unions the generals had tried to close down, and demonstrated in front of the newspaper where the editors had been arrested. You went into the *barrios* to take food to the hungry and find homes for the children whose parents had disappeared. Mother had to get a special shampoo when you came home with lice. You didn't care. You laughed and said, "I share everything."

"Eduardo," I pleaded, "you must give it up or they will come for you. Rosa told me students at the university are arrested just for belonging to a school organization, and they are never seen again." You would not be intimidated. A week later Isabela said she saw you standing on the steps of the university handing out flyers about the students' disappearance.

Father was furious. He jumped up from the dining room table and shouted at you, "Eduardo, you are putting us all in danger. Your mother, your sister, me. Stop this. You have no power over those savages, but believe me, they have power over *you*. Only be a little patient. The generals won't be there forever. He who lives by the sword, perishes by the sword."

"How many must die," you demanded, "waiting for that day to come?"

"Eduardo," Mother cried, "you are a holy fool. I

admire what you are doing, but it is suicide. How will you be able to help if they take you away? At least be more discreet. Do what you must do secretly; don't flaunt your deeds in their faces."

Father scolded Mother, "What kind of advice is that? They know everything. Knowing secrets is the generals' business."

Each evening I was terrified that you would not come home. Father would hold his medical journal in his hands but forget to turn the pages. Mother would sit with her pen suspended in the air. We'd wait. Finally Dichoso would bark and scratch at the front door, tail thumping. You would come into the house and we would breathe again.

At last you seemed to listen. You began to come home after your classes at the university instead of staying to demonstrate.

"I haven't seen your friends César and María," I said. "They don't stop by the house for you so that the three of you can go off on some secret mission."

You had no answer. You were restless and cross with me, but I said nothing, thinking that you missed your friends and were ashamed not to be supporting them. I was grateful and relieved that you had stopped your dangerous activities, and I gladly put up with the irritability. Then the police came for you and I realized you hadn't stopped at all.

After they took you away Father rushed out to talk with lawyers. He knew better than to go to the police. I helped Mother into the kitchen and made her sit down at the table while I put water on for tea. As I filled Mother's cup I was trembling so hard, I splashed boiling water on my hand. I didn't even feel it. I was like a small animal, threatened into a kind of shock, feeling nothing. Mother and I sat in our living room, which had never seemed so empty, our hands clasped, hanging on to each other. I looked into myself and found a tiny bit of courage I had no idea was there. I was furious with the police for taking you. I thought of them breaking into the homes of those who fought with you. I knew what I must do. I made some excuse to Mother and hurried into Father's study. I picked up the phone to warn your two closest friends. César thanked me and hurriedly put down the receiver. When I called María's house a strange voice answered. "Who is this?" he asked. "Who's there?" I was too late. María was *chupada*. Swallowed up by the military.

Eduardo, do you remember the summer you were eight? We had all gone swimming. Father ordered you to jump into the deep end of the pool instead of going down the steps. You stood there terrified, looking down at the circle of blue water, afraid that if you jumped, the water would wrap its arms about you, hold you, smother you. Father called you a baby. I saw him stride across the lawn meaning to push you in. I was only six and playing in the shallow water. I couldn't swim, but I forgot my own fears—I thought only of yours. I paddled into the deep water, nearly drowning. In rescuing me, Father forgot all about you.

Eduardo, I risked my life to save you that day, and I will risk it to save you now.

Eduardo

SILVIA, dear sister, your face was the last thing I saw before they put on the hood. That glimpse of you is with me. In my heart I will tell you everything, and the telling will give me strength.

They've thrown me into the car and pushed me onto the floor, slamming their feet on my back to keep me down. I'm trying to guess where we're heading, to remember the turns we make, to count the minutes, but terror crowds out thought and memory. The hood is kept on all the while so I see nothing. They refer to me as *el perro;* I am no more than a dog to them. But their wish not to be recognized gives me hope. Perhaps they know the day will come when they will be held accountable for their deeds.

I am dragged from the car and into a building whose stone walls are cold when I stumble against them.

They throw me into a room, a room with the smell of unwashed bodies and filthy toilets. It is the smell of terror. My hood is removed and an iron door slammed shut. The sound is of my world ending. Everything I care about is on the other side of that door.

I know where I am. I'm in the country of fear.

Here is the world in which I live. There is a narrow cot and in the corner of the room a tin bucket. A single lightbulb hangs from the ceiling and is always turned on. At first the light is comforting, and then it is a weapon. Every hour a slot in the door opens and someone peers in at me. I can see my own fear reflected in their eyes. There are screams from a nearby room. How brave will I be when it is my turn in that room?

At this moment I do not feel brave. My clothes are damp with sweat. I lose the strength to stand up, and I sink down on my cot. I think of you, Silvia. You warned me. You were afraid this would happen. But how can I have done otherwise? We can't live in a country where everyone is suspected and everyone is at risk. They tell writers what they can put in their books. They say this book must go and that one. A book that tells the truth about what is happening to Argentina is not allowed.

Over and over I see the terrible day they came into

my own department of experimental psychology. I was busy cleaning the cages of the mice, for Professor Bustamante was particular about the welfare of our animals. They had to be healthy and happy so they could run properly through the maze. It was a late afternoon on a Friday and I was eager for the weekend. Your birthday was the next day and I planned to wander through the antique stores in San Telmo to see if I could pick up a bit of the art deco jewelry you like so much.

Bustamante was short and a little fat, with a boyish face so innocent-looking that when he walked about the lab complaining loudly about our carelessness it was impossible to take him seriously. He did not even take his own temper tantrums seriously, for in the middle of a tirade he would begin to laugh at himself. And he was tenderness itself with the little mice. He called them his "*favoritos*" and fed them bits of cheese he brought from home. It pained him to give someone a poor grade, and on this day he was apologizing to one of the students for having awarded him a low test score. "It's for your own good, so that you will make an effort to improve," he pleaded.

At that moment a soldier strode into the laboratory. He stood there and stared at the little white mice, snug in their cages. Pointing to the maze, he asked Professor Bustamante, "What is that?"

"It's a maze," the professor said. "I would be glad to explain its workings to you." Though he was surprised to find a soldier in his lab, he was such a friendly man, I could see he was trying to make the young stranger feel at home. I could do nothing but stand there watching, wondering what would happen next and what I could do if it was something bad.

The soldier examined the water bottles and the pellets of food we gave the mice. He said, "You psychologists tinker with minds. You tell them what to think and what not to think. You influence thoughts." He walked over to the professor's untidy desk and began to rifle through his papers. He read out the title of a research paper, "'The Effect of Age on Directional Cognition.' First it is mice, but soon it is people," he said.

He found a copy of a study from a Russian university among Professor Bustamante's papers. "What is this Russian propaganda?" the soldier demanded.

The professor explained, "In the Russian university, young Russian mice and then older Russian mice are running through a maze as our mice do. The Russians are studying the results just as we are. That paper has nothing to do with Russian politics."

The soldier refused to believe him. Then, with the students staring helplessly, the soldier took Bustamante away. I will never forget the little gesture of apology he made to us students and his distraught look, a look that said in a second his world had been turned upside down. Without warning my professor had become one of the Desaparecidos.

"Eduardo," you told me, "forget about Bustamante. His disappearance has nothing to do with you, your protests will only get you into trouble."

But you did not know Bustamante as I did. He had always trusted everyone and now he will never trust again.

After that, I began to stand in front of the university with the others who were demonstrating against his disappearance. There were a dozen of us and we were all afraid. María and César and Ramón stood with me. Ramón's father was one of the Disappeared, and at the sight of the two soldiers who were posted at the university's entrance to watch us, Ramón's whole body would tremble. The soldiers would observe us just as we continued to observe the mice do their tricks in our lab. As we were in charge of the mice, the soldiers were in charge of us.

I told César, "We are not doing enough." A few of

us students decided to look about for something more effective to do, and joined a group of union workers demonstrating at a nearby factory. Their leader had been kidnapped by the generals, and members of their shop committees arrested.

At first the workers would have nothing to do with us because we were only students from the middle class and not *compañeros.* They suspected us of being spies for the government. Still, we came every day, proud of protesting with grown men and women. "You are little Innocents," they said. "You wear blue jeans like you are working men, though you have never done a day's work." They teased us in a friendly way, just as they made fun of one another, so that we would laugh to cover our fear.

They were just learning to trust us when Ramón Fratelli disappeared. I had been worried about my friend, for the police are like the hawk who singles out the weakest creature to pounce upon. I understood Ramón's fear. I had learned the details about his father when I stopped by Ramón's house one day to tell him the time of a demonstration. Ramón was not at home, but his mother and his sister, Teresa, invited me in for a cool drink. They told me that Señor Fratelli was a reporter who had disappeared mysteriously while covering an investigation of the corruption in the government's awarding of contracts.

The Fratellis, like many in Buenos Aires, were of Italian rather than Spanish decent. The mother was a large comfortable woman who was clearly the rock of the family. She accepted the disappearance of her husband as one would accept an earthquake or a typhoon, enduring while questioning neither man nor God. Suffering, Silvia, as you and Mother and Father must now be suffering.

Ramón's sister was delicate with a pale face and long dark hair. Her eyes were large and fringed with sooty lashes. She had the look of a fairy creature peering out from amongst the trees in some enchanted forest. Unlike Señora Fratelli, she appeared to be looking everywhere for answers, terrified that she might find them. Impulsively I put an arm around her shoulder. I wanted to protect her, to keep her from harm. For just a moment I questioned the risk Ramón was taking when he had the responsibility for his mother and sister, but then I told myself nothing could be more important than fighting against what was happening to our country.

The señora said, "Eduardo, I beg you to find a way to stop my son from all this political activity. After what has happened to Señor Fratelli, the police will have their eye on Ramón. He is a sensitive boy, and I see how he suffers with anxiety. He feels he must do what his father did. I have lost my husband. It would kill me to lose my son as well."

Teresa laid her hand as light as a leaf on my arm. "I know that you are his friend. Is there no way you can keep him from this foolishness? It's a danger to *all* of you."

But I had not listened to my family, and I did not listen to the Fratellis.

A week later when Ramón did not turn up to demonstrate with us, I went at once to the Fratelli home and found his mother turned to stone and Teresa in tears.

Teresa said, "Last night just before midnight a carload of soldiers broke down our door and took Ramón away. We have asked everywhere, but no one will talk with us. Everyone is afraid."

Her mother was beyond speech.

My friend was in the hands of the generals and we would all be suspected now. Of all of us Ramón was the most easily intimidated. I guessed he would be so terrified, he would not long hold out against torture. He would begin to tell who his comrades were.

I tried to comfort the Fratellis. "It was most likely a mistake. After a few questions Ramón is sure to be returned." The señora wanted to believe me, as one believes in many things one knows are false, but Teresa said nothing, only crying silently, her face turned away so her mother would not see her tears.

That next week two of the students and one of the leaders of the union strike were arrested. I waited for my own arrest or that of María or César, but nothing happened. Had Ramón betrayed some but not others? I told María and César of my concerns. We were ashamed for Ramón, yet we did not know if under torture we might not do the same. I wanted to believe I would be brave. Now, as I listen in my cell to cries of pain, I have little faith in my courage.

María, César, and I gave thanks that so far we had been spared, and we continued to demonstrate with the workers even though we knew that at any moment the police might come for us. Some among the union leaders frightened me. I guessed their belief in their cause came less from conviction than hate for those in authority. They whispered among themselves so that we students could not hear. One of them made friends with me. I was pleased when he first approached me. Now I call him the Jackal, for he was an animal who with his bloodthirsty schemes existed on carrion, the dead and decaying flesh of his victims.

The others seemed to separate themselves from the Jackal, but I felt superior that one of the union leaders had made a comrade of me. After one of our demonstrations he invited me to join him for a coffee, so I went along, swaggering a little. I had been singled out as someone to be trusted. When María and César warned me about the man, I thought they were jealous.

The Jackal took me to a little café near the factory. A waiter with a surly manner poured the coffee into dirty cups and wandered off. The Jackal said, "Tell me a little about yourself. How did you come to be involved in our demonstrations? You could be off having a good time like the rest of the students."

"No, no. I'm not interested in a meaningless life. I want to help my country. I want to get rid of the generals and bring democracy back to Argentina." Eagerly I told him, "I am one of you, a true compañero. I have demonstrated at the university and I write articles about the cruelty of the generals and how their government must be overturned."

"And what do you do with these essays?" he asked. He asked it casually, as if it did not matter to him one way or the other.

"Of course at present they can't be published because of the censorship, but one day they will be." I was very proud of what I had written.

"I'd be interested in reading them," he said. This surprised me, for I had thought the Jackal a man who would reach for knives and guns before he would turn to words.

I went on talking about myself and our family, not noticing the Jackal's silence about himself. When I paused for a breath, he said, "I saw at once you were smarter than your fellow students and more dedicated to our cause. How would you like to take on a very special, very secret mission for us?"

I was excited. "Yes, of course," I agreed. "I will do anything."

Even more gratifying, he said, "Let me have those articles you say you have written. I'd like to keep them for a day or two and show them to a friend who prints an underground newspaper. They're exactly what the man is looking for."

I did not like having the articles out of my hands, but I was flattered, and I promised to bring them to him at once.

"One more thing," he said. "You must stop the demonstrating. We need you to be away from the eyes of the police. Say nothing. Do nothing. Wait until you are contacted."

I was full of importance; I thought of myself as a secret agent. When César asked, "How come you aren't coming to demonstrate today?" I made up a story about how my family had finally convinced me to give up the protests. When I saw I had fallen in his eyes, I could not help but give him a hint. "Anyhow, there are more important jobs to be done, but I can't talk about them." César was impressed.

As the days went on I waited eagerly for someone to contact me, wondering what crucial task I would be called upon to perform. When I saw the other students demonstrating, talking about what they had done and what they would do next, I felt left out. At home, Silvia, you noticed that I no longer went with César and María, and you were relieved and pleased. You thought I had listened to you and to Father and Mother.

At last the Jackal summoned me to the small out-of-the-way café where we had gone before. He announced, "Eduardo, the time has come for your important mission."

My heart raced. Finally I would begin. Finally I would make a difference. "What am I to do?"

The Jackal said, "We have learned a friend of yours, Ramón Fratelli, who was picked up by the soldiers, has named his comrades. Ramón was seen in a car with soldiers pointing out not only students, but one of the leaders of our union. We can't let that go unpunished."

"But Ramón is in prison," I said. I couldn't imagine a greater punishment.

"Ah, but his family is not," the Jackal said.

I didn't understand. "There is only his mother and sister. His father has disappeared." At once I was on my guard, thinking of Teresa. Why was he talking of the Fratellis?

"We need to send a lesson to informers that betrayal will have consequences."

I still didn't follow him. "You want me to tell his family what Ramón has done? I could not punish them like that."

"That would be a very weak lesson. We have something else in mind." There was a look of excitement in the Jackal's eyes, as if a wish dear to him was about to be granted. "You know the family, don't you? You have been in their home."

"Yes, of course. He was one of us." It did not occur to me to wonder how he knew this. Soon it would be obvious they had been watching me.

"Ramón's family trusts you?"

"Yes, I suppose so; yes, of course. I am sure they trust me." It was wrenching to think of what Ramón's family must be going through. What he did in betraying his friends was a terrible thing, but it wasn't his family's fault. I told the Jackal that.

"This is a war," he said. "There will always be innocent victims. That is the nature of war. I picked you out because I thought you understood such things."

I could hardly take his words in. What was he asking of me? "Tell me what you want me to do."

"You have only to deliver a package. There will be no danger to you and no one to connect you with what will happen."

I could barely get the words out. "You are asking me to take a bomb into the Fratellis' house."

"You told me you were serious about defeating the generals. I took you at your word. I thought you understood that to destroy them we must be as strong as they are. Instead I find you are only a child, a timid pretender. Ramón's betrayal has put us into the hands of the enemy. We must make an example of him—we can't have our people telling all they know when they are arrested. But if it will protect a mother or a sister, they will find the strength to endure torture."

"You want us to fight terror by becoming terrorists ourselves. You can call me a coward—I would never do such a thing."

"I think you will."

"Never." I was a fool to believe I had been singled out because I was superior in some way. They had simply guessed how easily I would be flattered, how anxious I was for their approval. "If I do what you want, our side will be as bad as the generals. Then Argentina would suffer under two evils, one against the other with nothing to choose between."

The Jackal became livid. "Don't be one of those idiots who believe the end does not justify the means. You are in an army now and you must follow orders. You have no choice. "

"I do have a choice."

"Then *my* choice would be to turn over your articles to the generals so that they can see just what you think of their government."

How could I have been so stupid not to see this trap he had set for me? I was furious with him and with myself. Even worse, Ramón's betrayal came after torture; *my* betrayal was the result of my conceit and self-importance. Whichever way I turned I faced danger and threat.

The Jackal was watching me. But what he didn't see, dear sister, and what you would have known at once, was that I would die before I did what he wished.

Silvia

DEAR Eduardo, we are not alone in our sorrow over your arrest. The more we reach out to find you, the more we find others who are also suffering. There are so many, we wonder if our arms can embrace them all. Do you remember how you and I loved to watch puppet shows, believing the puppets were real, wondering where the characters went when they vanished beneath the stage? Argentina is like a giant puppet show with some reckless puppeteer making first one character disappear and then another. We see only the disappearances and never the hands that have snatched us from the stage.

It was the military police who took you away, so Father went to the army's first command and talked with the general there. "Doctor Díaz, you have my sympathy, but no one in the military would enter the home of an Argentinean citizen. Of course I will make inquiries, but I assure you such a thing is impossible. These are difficult times, and so we must rally around our country. It is unfortunate that your son should support those at the university and in the unions who oppose our government." Father said the general spoke in a dismissive tone and would not meet his eye.

Mother asked, "How did the general know about Eduardo's activities?"

Father shook his head. "I never said a word."

So we knew they had you.

Still, Father went to the municipal police, who denied knowing anything about your arrest. "This is an unruly country," the lieutenant said. "Probably they were guerrillas wanting to get some ransom money. No doubt you will hear from them with a demand. By all means let us know if that happens."

Finally, in our desperation, Father went to the cathedral to speak with the bishop. "We are losing our children," the bishop said. "Still it is wrong to oppose the state as they do. I am very sorry for you, but your son should have chosen better friends." But another priest, young Father Paul, was waiting in the darkened church and motioned Father into the confessional, where they would not be seen. In a low voice he whispered, "There is a small band of priests who are dedicated to getting information about Los Desaparecidos. Give me a picture of your son. We will see what we can do."

The priest took the picture of you that Father had brought for the bishop. "Of course what we do is dangerous," Father Paul said. "Already two of our group have themselves been arrested. But we are not afraid. Surely we have God on our side."

Because of her poetry, Mother knows writers from other countries who are members of an international commission on human rights; one of them has written an article about the disappearances. When Mother contacted the woman, she said, "Many people have approached the commission for help, but we can do very little, for the Argentinean government will not cooperate with us."

So there was no one to help us. Instead, we learned the stories of hundreds of other victims. To our own worry was added the sorrow of many others. Mothers and fathers were searching for their children, wives for their husbands and husbands for their wives. One mother said both of her children had been taken, "Students like yourself," she said, and embraced me as if I were her daughter. When I told her about you I said I wished I had been taken too so that we could give each other courage. She covered my hand with hers. "Thank God that you were spared so that you can help your parents find your brother, whether he is alive or dead." There was little to give me hope in words like that.

But now, my hope returns as I think of what she said. I was spared so that I might help find you. I say nothing to Mother and Father, but I am resolved to free you, and I have a scheme.

You know how we loved spy films, how the first English words we learned were from the subtitles of American mystery movies. *Danger* was one of those words, and *suspicion,* and *death*. When we made up our own spy games, we took turns being the enemy and learning each other's secrets. We followed each other when we went out, slipping behind trees and hiding in doorways. I knew where in your room you kept your girlfriend's letter, and you knew in which drawer I hid the lipstick Mother couldn't find.

The mystery movies taught us that you could fool people. You could enter into their lives pretending you were someone you were not. You would be trusted and then you would carry out your scheme. Eduardo, you would see only the danger, but I see how I can free you. I have even chosen the boy I will use to carry out my plan.

You always teased me about the boys who followed me around. "Like bees after honey," you said. You would ask, "What poor fool sent you those flowers? Whose heart are you breaking today?"

Once when Mother and I were shopping for clothes, a department store manager asked if I would like to take up modeling. And you remember last year the professor at the art school begged me to come and pose for the students. "Just your face," he had said, "it is the face of a Madonna." But I was too self-conscious. I blushed and said, "I'm afraid my studies will not allow me the time."

Now I will use my looks for something more useful than walking up and down a runway or sitting for artists. I will do whatever it takes to make Norberto fall in love with me. I will make him care so much for me that he will ask his father for your freedom. I am desperate enough, Eduardo, to hope I can touch the heart of someone who you would say has no heart. If you were here you would surely find a way to keep me from carrying out my plan, but this letter will not reach you and you cannot stop me.

Tonight, Friday, I have made an excuse to Rosa and Isabela. I'm going by myself to the disco where I danced with Norberto. I spend hours doing my hair in a new way and choose a dress that is provocative without being in poor taste. I look about as I enter the disco as if I am meeting someone. At once Norberto hurries up to me. "Come and join our table," he says, "while you wait for your friends." Just as I remembered, Norberto is a large, beefy boy. There is a meatiness to him that makes me think of a plate too filled with food. I can see he is aware of his father's importance, for he swaggers a little. He leads me to a table he shares with two other boys and their dates. The boys regard me with interest, moving over to make room for me. The girl who must be Norberto's date glares at me. The other girls give me a quick appraisal and turn away.

In the past the discos were exciting, but after they took you away, Eduardo, it is a small hell to be here and I feel a wave of nausea at the thought of all of those evenings I spent so foolishly.

Norberto looks at me. "What's the matter? Aren't you feeling well?"

"Yes, of course," I answer quickly. "Why don't we dance?"

He is on his feet at once, taking my hand to lead me onto the floor. His touch disgusts me; it is all I can do not to pull away. They are playing a tango and he holds me close. I think that when he leaves me tonight, he will go home to his father, General López, the man who ordered your arrest, and I want to run from the room. I begin to doubt that I can carry on this charade long enough to reach his heart. I close my eyes and think only of you, of what you are going through and how this will save you. When the tango is finished I plead thirst and Norberto leads me back to the table. He is drinking beer and wants to order one for me, but I ask for a Coke.

"You'll never have any fun that way," he says.

"I don't need beer to have fun," I tell him, and give him what I hope is a warm smile. He squeezes my arm. He tells me he likes my dress and the way I do my hair. He watches me like a fox watching a rabbit.

Norberto and the two other boys discuss *fútbol*. Argentina is going to host the World Cup soccer matches next year. Norberto and his friends have all played on local teams. While they get into an argument over whether Pelé or DiStefano was the greater player, the three girls bend their heads together to discuss the shops where they buy shoes.

The shifting lights, the conversations that have to be shouted to be heard over the loud music, the warmth of the room from all the bodies, and the smell of cigarettes and beer are like a bad play in which I have only a silent walk-on part.

Left to myself I have time to consider the awful danger of what I am doing. Norberto is no fool. If he sees that I am using him he may turn on me. But I tell myself I will discover in Norberto that small seed of goodness that is surely in everyone, and I will nourish it and make it flower, pushing through the dark evil that is his father.

I look over at Norberto. His face is flushed and he is emphasizing his point by pounding on the table with his beer bottle. There is some argument about the scoring on a match. "You don't know what you are talking about," he is shouting at the other two boys. They shrug good-naturedly and let it go, but Norberto keeps pounding on the table. I see that he must always be right. If someone disagrees with him he bullies them. I guess that they give in because they know General López is one of the most dangerous men in Argentina.

It is Norberto's father, General López, whom I have singled out to free you.

A hand on my shoulder makes me look up. I see Isabela, and Rosa with her. Isabela gives me a look of disbelief. Norberto is about to make room for them when Rosa says in an icy voice, "No, thank you. We just wanted to say hello to Silvia." With that they leave to take a table on the other side of the room. I wait a few minutes and then make an excuse to go to the restroom. Norberto and the other two are back to their fútbol discussion and pay no attention.

I make my way across the room.

"You told us you couldn't come tonight," Rosa says.

"Something changed," I reply quietly.

"*You've* changed," Rosa says. "You know Norberto is General López's son. We said we weren't going to have anything to do with him."

"He may be the son, but he's not the general," I say. "It's unfair to criticize him for what his father does."

"Does he disagree with his father, then?" Isabela asks.

"We haven't discussed politics." From the expressions on their faces I see they are confused and hurt. I want to whisper in their ears, "Only trust me," but I don't dare. "Look, I have to go. I'm sorry about tonight."

I dance every dance with Norberto. The girl he had been with sulks, but he pays her no attention; she might have been a stranger. When one of the other boys, ignoring his girlfriend's cold stare, asks me to dance with him, Norberto gives a nasty laugh and says, "She's mine."

So that is what I have become—Norberto's property.

For a moment I think of making some excuse and leaving, for I feel I am entering a series of caves, making my way down one dark tunnel to another with no direction and no escape. But Norberto is attentive. He sees that my glass is filled, orders a flan topped with *dulce de leche* for me. At the end of the evening he insists on taking me home. In working out my scheme I had planned to be in control, but shut with him in his car, I feel control slipping away.

Norberto is an aggressive driver. He is his own army laying siege to every car on the road, conquering it and battling on to overtake the next one.

When we reach our house Norberto says, "Let me drive you to Tigre this weekend to meet my parents. They are staying in their summer place for a few weeks and I always go up to see them on Sundays."

I try to picture a happy family scene. Instead I

imagine General López in the middle of his family like a spider in the middle of a web.

After a moment Norberto asks, "Will you come?"

I am terrified of meeting the general, but I tell myself that in Norberto's home I will see another side of him, a gentler side. I will find the Norberto I need. "Yes, I'd like that," I say.

As he tries to take me in his arms, I spring out of the car.

"What's the matter?" he asks in a hurt voice. "I thought you liked me."

I lean in the car window and kiss him good night. He tastes of stale beer and cigarettes.

Eduardo, I am doing this for you.

Eduardo

MY dear Silvia, this is what I have learned. In this place my body is not my own. The body I have taken such care of all these years, washing it and clothing it, feeding and exercising it, has been taken from me. It belongs to General Remos, who sends for me each morning—at least I think it is morning, for there is no window in my cell, and the bulb that hangs from the ceiling is my sun and moon. I am feeble, for I am given nothing to eat but a little bread or thin soup, which is brought to me sporadically or not at all.

Hunger meddles with my every thought. A guard comes for me and I am led blindfolded to a room. I stand with my arms twisted around to the back and handcuffed. My arms feel as if they have been torn from my shoulders. In my weakness I weave a little from side to side. General Remos gives an order and someone strikes me. I fall exhausted to the floor and someone throws water on me. General Remos decides what my body will do.

I can see from the general's stripes that he has a high rank. He asks the same questions over and over. He sounds bored and angry, as if he doesn't want to be there, but at the same time being there is important to him. Some of the questions I expect. "Who worked with you against the government? Who has been disloyal at the university? At the trade union?"

General Remos is very angry. He says, "You may as well know that one of your so-called friends betrayed you. What is more, we have the treasonous articles you wrote."

I say, "It is not treason to love your country. I am someone who hates what is happening to Argentina and I say so."

A guard hits me about the shoulders with a rubber truncheon. The truncheon lands on the back of my neck and I lose consciousness. As I come to, I hear a voice through the pain. The voice says, "I am a doctor. Can you hear me?" I am grateful. Someone to care for me. I mumble, "Yes."

The doctor says, "He's fine, you can go ahead, just watch where you strike him."

The words of the doctor hurt more than any blow. All my life I have seen my father practice his profession to help others. He is a strong man and brusque in behavior, but his eyes and his fingers are always tender. He is giving his life to end the suffering of others. Once I tried to help Dichoso after he caught his foot in a trap set for rats, but my dog snarled and showed his teeth. He trusted only Father's tenderness.

That a doctor would aid the generals destroys all my hope. If they have the power to seduce a doctor to do the very opposite of what his profession calls for, they have more power than even I thought, and I am utterly helpless against it. Still, I tell myself that every minute I resist is a minute more for César and María and the others to escape before the day I name them. And I am sure that day will come, for I have heard the screams of those whose torture must be worse than blows with a truncheon. Impatience creeps into the voice of my inquisitor. "You are a fool to think you can outlast me," he says. The increase in the strikes tells me my day will soon arrive.

I am brought back to my prison cell and given a push that lands me on the floor. I dread the cell, for worse than the truncheon is the pain of loneliness. Anything can be borne if it is not borne alone. Just then I hear tapping noises from the adjoining cell. I put my arms against the cold concrete wall and embrace it. The taps are deliberate and come in a series. After a minute I know what they are—the universal language of prisoners. I learned of it first in Arthur Koestler's book *Darkness at Noon,* a story of a Russian prison. All over the world, where prisoners sit alone in their cells, they rely on a kind of code. It would take forever to tap out each letter of the alphabet, but if you make a little box of five rows, with the alphabet divided amongst them, you can tap out the row and then the letter. I hear one tap for the first row and then three taps for the third letter in that row. This gives C. My comrade keeps tapping until he has spelled out a word: courage. I tap back the same message. At that moment, no one in my whole life, not Mother or Father or even you, Silvia, is dearer to me. Not to be alone is as good as having an army on my side. A bond with another prisoner will help to protect me against the worst they can do.

The worst soon comes.

I am dragged back to the inquisitor. General Remos asks again and again what I know, and when I say I know nothing it is time for the *picana,* the electric cattle prod. They tie me to a table and splash me with water so that the electric shocks will be more painful. The picana is applied to the most vulnerable parts of my body. My torturers might be cutting with pleasure into the tenderest section of a cut of beef, savoring the way the knife slices easily into the meat and the blood pools on the plate. At first the electric prod only stings. Then it burns. A voice that no longer belongs to me screams. Again the doctor comes, for they do not want me to die, then the questions all over again. Then the picana. I will not speak of this again.

I return to the cell and the tapping. At first I am unable to concentrate, but finally I make out the message: pity. I remember words I had read by the Russian writer Dostoevsky: "Man cannot live without pity." I think of all the years and all the millions of people who have cried out for pity. Now I am lost among them.

Alone and terrified of what will come, I flee to the past—for the past is all I have and maybe all I will ever have. I look about in my memories to make a book to read, for I have come to realize that our lives are but books to read and reread. We cross out and add and finally we come up with happy endings. I am desperate for a happy ending.

◆ ◆ ◆

Remember, Silvia, the time you and I went with Mother and Father to visit Uncle Julio at his *estancia*? You were ten and I was thirteen. How I had bragged at school about our uncle who owned a ranch and five hundred head of cattle. To keep my mind busy I try to rebuild every inch of the two hours of travel from our busy city of Buenos Aires to the little town of San Antonio de Areco. Just before we made the visit I had read the great Argentinean poem "Martín Fierro," about the life of the cowboy gauchos on the pampas, how they tended the cattle by day, and by night fought one another to the death with their *facónes,* knives, in vengeful quarrels. They slept on the ground with no shelter but the heaven and the stars above. I remember how thrilled and excited I was at the prospect of meeting real gauchos. We crossed the River Areco on an old bridge and drove through the countryside with its green fields and vast spaces like great empty rooms. Suddenly cities seemed unnecessary, even foolish.

Uncle Julio's *casco* with its wings and terraces and porches was spread across a wide green lawn. I wanted to go immediately to the ranch to see the five hundred cattle, but first we had a luncheon. I remember the two-story dining hall with its great beams, and how you embarrassed Father by weeping for the deer and wild boar whose heads were nailed to the white-washed walls. Silvia, you were always someone to feel another's pain. I know you are thinking of me now.

We sat at the table for what seemed hours as the servants brought in trays of enormous barbequed steak—I was afraid there would be no cows left on the ranch for me to see. At last Uncle Julio said, "Come along now and I'll show you some fine cattle." He put me into a Jeep and drove out onto the fields. I was still expecting gauchos with wide pants and belts of silver, and tucked into the belt, the deadly facón. Instead, the gauchos wore blue jeans and leather belts and I saw no knives; nevertheless, looking out over the grasslands that stretched to the horizon, I was sure theirs was the life I wanted.

Shyly I asked Uncle Julio, "Could I come and work for you?"

He said, "I'll keep a place for you, Eduardo, but first you must finish school and go to university. When you graduate, if you still wish to come, you will be welcome. Of course, you must be content to sleep in the dormitory with two dozen gauchos and to get up before daylight and go to bed with the sun."

"*Sí, sí,*" I eagerly assented. I brought home the horns

from one of the steers and triumphantly put them up on the wall of my bedroom as a promise.

I gave up the dream of working on a ranch long ago, but now it comes back to me in my cell and I make use of it. I empty myself of fear by filling each second imagining what that life might be. I picture the dormitory where we gauchos sleep, I hear the sounds of men stirring on their cots, turning over, snoring, mumbling to themselves as they live in their dreams. I see the first rays of the sun lighten the windows and the men, grumbling and swearing at another day of hard work, rolling out of bed, pulling on shirts and jeans, stumbling half asleep to their breakfast of steak. "It gives them the strength for the day's work," Uncle Julio had said.

Minute by minute I go through their day, adding and subtracting. One day all is peaceful but another day some word is taken for an insult and there is a fight, with the gauchos taking sides and plotting revenge. In my imagination I live each day for the night, when I steal out of the dormitory and lie alone under the heavens, the Southern Cross overhead in a black sea of stars, the last thing I see before I close my eyes and sleep. For I can't sleep shut into this coffin of concrete with no sky above me, and no star but the cruel lightbulb.

◆ ◆ ◆

I and the prisoner in the cell next to me are cautious with our tapping, reluctant to give even our names, unsure if we have been placed next to each other to gain incriminating evidence. But the need to communicate with a fellow human being is strong. I tap, "Student," and he taps, "Me too, university."

We are both students at the university. With a shudder I think of César and other students who demonstrated with me. I take a chance and tap my name, Eduardo. He taps back, Ramón. I can't breathe. I tell myself Ramón is a common name, that it is impossible for this to be the Ramón who once was my friend, who stood together with me against the generals, who distributed the leaflets I wrote, and then drove about with the soldiers to turn me in. I draw away from the wall, but I have to know. "A sister," I tap, "Silvia."

"Teresa," he taps, and the taps come fast. "Eduardo. Is it you? Is my family safe?" I catch my breath. I want to tell Ramón that I have risked my life to protect them. But is he to be trusted? Would any message I tap be told to Remos? I want to let Ramón know that Teresa and his mother have escaped, but have they? And if they haven't, my mentioning them might mean trouble. I am unsure of my motive. Do I really think it dangerous to mention Teresa and her mother's name, or do I want to punish Ramón for his part in my imprisonment? For either reason or both, I don't respond, leaving this boy who may be my friend with silence in which to nourish his fear.

I am learning cruelty.

Silvia

EDUARDO, while I am trying to make Norberto care enough for me to do what I ask, Mother goes each day to the Plaza de Mayo. The mothers are there to protest the disappearance of their loved ones. Every afternoon they gather at the plaza to march around and around the pyramid at its center, the pyramid that was built to commemorate Argentina's freedom from Spain, and stands there beside the mothers, a reminder of why they march. On the east side of the plaza, looming over the marchers, is Casa Rosada. In the Pink House is the office of General Videla, the president of Argentina. Does he have any regrets when he looks down from his windows? At end of the plaza is the old jail with its barred windows. On the balcony of the jail armed soldiers look out at the women like hawks watching a flock of small birds, picking and choosing who next to pounce upon.

Mother has joined the marchers, and Saturday afternoon I go with her. Father doesn't know about her marching; Mother says it would only be one more worry for him. She comes home from the marches and shuts herself in her room. She is putting the stories of the women into poems. "The stories must be saved," she says. "If the children can't be saved, then we will be a witness to their disappearance. If I can find a way to publish those poems secretly, I will."

A few months ago there were only a few women marching; now there are over a hundred. They wear white kerchiefs tied over their hair and walk arm in arm, many carrying pictures of their vanished children. Mother boldly marches with your picture, Eduardo, the newspaper picture of you protesting on the steps of the university. The determined look on your face makes it seem that you are marching too.

In the official newspaper the women are called *Las Locas de la Plaza de Mayo,* the crazies of the Plaza de Mayo. But I stand there amazed. You know what a quiet person Mother is, keeping to herself, her mind always busy on the next poem. In a room full of people she is always close to the door as if ready to flee. Marching was the last thing I expected of her, but she has never missed an afternoon. In the evenings she brings home to me the stories of the women she marches with. They are like our own story, a son or daughter swept up by police or the military and put in jails—or worse, secretly executed.

The sun is hot on this afternoon and Mother pauses for a moment to join me where I am standing in the shade. Her friend Señora Suárez comes with her, and Mother introduces me. It was Señora Suárez's daughter, Alma, who once published Mother's poems. Alma's magazine was not afraid to print articles criticizing the generals. Señora Suárez is so thin, I could close my fingers around her wrists. Her fleshless elbows are sharp points and her dress hangs on her. She tells me the story of her daughter.

"Alma was pregnant when she was picked up," Señora Suárez says. "She had her baby in jail and we learned from someone who had been there with Alma that her baby was taken. We don't know where it is. My grandchild has disappeared."

Mother says, "Not only Alma. Señora Suárez and I hear the same stories from other mothers. Babies and even young children are taken from parents who are arrested. The military tries to justify these kidnappings. They say, 'Those parents have defied the government, and their children will grow up to be like their parents, a danger to the state. We find better homes for them. We give them to families who love this country.' So the babies and the little children are snatched from their imprisoned mothers and given to 'patriotic' families, often to military families who want children and can't have them. The mothers never see them again."

Señora Suárez says, "Not only has Alma been stolen from me, but my grandchild will grow up in a family that will teach the child to hate her mother and father and me and all we stand for."

Suddenly a policeman who has been watching the marchers swoops down on a woman and drags her away. The other marchers do not stop, they merely close their ranks.

"What will happen to that woman?" I ask.

Señora Suárez tells us, "They will take her to the police station. This is one more attempt to harass us. They send photographers to take our pictures and spies to march with us."

"How can you tell who the spies are?" I ask.

"Ah, Silvia," Mother says, "you have only to look into the eyes of a mother to find the sorrow. There is no such sorrow in the eyes of the spies. Only cold deceit."

Mother and Señora Suárez are back marching

when a man comes up to the women and screams, "Traitors!" He picks up a small stone from the ground and hurls it at them. The stone glances off the shoulder of one of the mothers and falls to the ground. The marchers take no notice. Late in the afternoon a young boy comes with his guitar and sings melancholy songs in the voice of an angel.

On the way home Mother says something that breaks my heart. "Silvia, you must have noticed, some of the daughters of the mothers march arm in arm with the mothers. I thought for Eduardo's sake you might like to march with me. I know how you grieve for him."

Eduardo, what could I reply? Of course I longed to take Mother's arm and march with her. But I could not. Suppose Norberto saw me? At once he would be suspicious. My whole plan would fall to pieces, and I am sure it is the only way to bring you back to us.

"Mother," I said, the words as bitter to me as any I have spoken, "I had better not. Just now the police are keeping an eye on all the students."

"Yes," Mother said. "Yes, I understand. It is certainly best to be cautious."

Cautious. To me that was a hateful world. Cautious, when I am risking everything in what I plan, but I could not tell Mother. I can only endure her disappointment in her timid daughter.

I don't sleep. I cannot stop thinking of you, Eduardo, and of Señora Suárez and her daughter and grandchild. Do you remember Mother reading to us "The Deeds of Elal," the fable of Argentina's beginning? Do you remember the giant, Goshge, who would come every night to devour a child? Then the hero, Elal, changed himself into a horsefly, made his way into the stomach of the giant, and bit him so hard that the giant was vanquished. Eduardo, we need an Elal now to destroy the evil giants who are devouring our Disappeared.

At last the dawn comes and I get up and dress. This is the day that I will drive with Norberto to his family's place in Tigre. I make some excuse to Mother and Father about spending the day with Isabela. To Norberto, who wanted to pick me up at home, I said, "My parents would never let me spend the day at Tigre with a boy." Which is true.

I meet him at a small café near the Plaza del Congreso. I can't tell one make of car from another, but Norberto's car is shiny, black, and large, like a great beetle scurrying along the road. I have worn my best summer dress, the blue one with the halter neckline and the full skirt. You said the dress made me look like a movie star. As I slip into the seat beside Norberto I see his admiring look. We head north along the coast. I have never been to Tigre, but I know it for a sleepy port where the jungle streams from inland Argentina flow into the delta and out to sea. Norberto is full of chatter about movies he has seen.

"I want to see *Rocky* again and I'll take you with me to see it. It's about this scheme to make a winner out of a loser who never got anywhere in a boxing match. The match is just for publicity, but he wins anyhow. There's some terrific boxing, I mean he really takes a beating. You have to see *Taxi Driver* too. It's about a Vietnam veteran who drives a taxi in a part of New York like our La Boca and he goes crazy and becomes a killer. There's this great scene when blood spatters everywhere."

I am frightened. I can't look at Norberto without thinking of everything for which his father is responsible, but I try to convince myself that Norberto is just a small boy who likes to pretend he is tough. He is a child pretending to be a gangster and going "bang, bang" with an imaginary gun. Besides, I am relieved to have Norberto do all the talking, for I worry about my every word, afraid I will give myself away.

From time to time Norberto reaches over and pats my leg for emphasis. I steel myself to keep from flinching. In spite of my disgust, I feel a little sorry for Norberto and the way he is so anxious to make himself liked. I think when he was young he must have been that boy no one picked for their team. He would have stood on the sidelines, waiting and hoping while others were chosen. All that would have changed when his father became an important and feared man and the family became so rich that Norberto could buy himself friends.

In Tigre we park the car and are met at the Estación Fluvial by a uniformed boatman and a launch with the general's name stenciled on the bow. The launch travels through a maze of canals that make up the delta of the Paraná River. The river is the color of earth and I can't see into it. We pass dense tangles of trees and huts on stilts and then surprisingly large homes tucked onto islands in the river. We round a curve and I see the ghostly vision of a large mansion. The launch ties up at the mansion's dock and Norberto helps me off. "It's Papá's little getaway," he says, smiling at my openmouthed amazement.

As we walk up the path to the mansion, Norberto says, "Papá and Mamá always come down on the weekends."

I have heard General López is a strong and dynamic man, a soldier who has crushed revolutions and destroyed his enemies. So I am not prepared for the man who comes toward us. He is leaning on a cane and very thin, like someone from whom too much has been taken. In spite of the warm weather and the sun, he is pale, the transparent pale of grubs who live underground. I see that the man is ill. Immediately I worry. If something should happen to the general my plan will come to nothing.

I am relieved to see the proud and loving look he gives Norberto. The more he cares for his son, the more it will suit my purpose. "Ah, so you are my son Norberto's new friend?" he says to me. "You are very welcome. Come in, come in. Norberto will show you around. I would claim the pleasure for myself, but just now I'm a little tired." I had worried that the general might know who I was, but our last name, Díaz, is a common one and there is nothing but courtesy in his manner toward me.

A moment later a woman who must be Norberto's mother embraces her son and then hurries to her husband. She is a tall woman, her black hair pulled mercilessly back from her face. Her dark eyes are hooded like shades pulled down to keep one from seeing into a room. "Arturo," she says to the general, "what are you doing up? This is your time to rest." She turns to me. "You're Silvia. Our son has spoken of you." Señora López takes my hand. "We are so pleased Norberto has a young woman friend. I hope you will have a civilizing effect upon my son. He is too much with boys his age who think of nothing but fighting and getting into trouble. You will excuse me if I see to my husband. The general refuses to take proper care of himself." In a tone full of irony she adds, "If my husband should become ill, there would be no one to fill the prisons of Argentina."

I have trouble concealing my shock. The general flushes. He starts to make an angry answer, but Señora López interrupts him. "Norberto, take Silvia out to the terrace, where it is cool."

The terrace looks out across a wide lawn to the river. It is paved in green tiles the color of the grass and furnished with comfortable chairs and a long table. I imagine many evenings of family suppers here, or perhaps the general's fellow officers come to plot someone's destruction. Then I look again. Among the tall grasses around the terrace is a hodgepodge of cages, some large, some small, all suspended on poles. Trapped in the cages are a variety of birds. Seeing my interest, Norberto says, "They're mine. I catch them. Come and see."

The largest of the cages, though certainly not large enough for the poor bird imprisoned within, holds a great white creature with a long yellow bill and black feet. Its neck is folded into an S shape. As we get closer it flaps its wings as if about to take flight, but the cage is only large enough for it to dance a bit from side to side. "A great egret," Norberto says. "Not very rare, but look at this one." In a nearby cage is a small bird with a red breast. "Lesser red-breasted meadowlark. It's an accidental. You almost never see them here. It's difficult to tell it from a long-tailed meadowlark. I was lucky to get it. After I had a glimpse of it I had the boys out with nets for a week." With great pride Norberto says, "I've reported it to the ornithological society. In their newsletter they will mention my name."

Some of the cages imprison owls and nighthawks. Last year our English class read *Julius Caesar,* and I can't help shuddering as I think of Shakespeare's lines: "Yesterday the bird of night did sit, even at noonday, upon the market place, hooting and shrieking."

Norberto takes my arm and pulls me from cage to cage, identifying the captives. He tells me just where in the country each bird comes from and where they migrate to in the winter. He knows the life history of each of his prisoners. "I like studying them," he says. "I wouldn't mind being an ornithologist, but my father wants me to go into the army."

I feel a little sorry for Norberto and his frustrated wishes. Still, I am miserable seeing the birds jailed in their meager cells. I ask, "Why have you put all these birds into cages?"

"The better to study them. Why shouldn't I do what I want with them; they were on our property. Anyhow, they're better off here than they would be in the wild. They get fed without having to do a thing, and as long as they're in their cages nothing can harm them. I'm doing them a favor."

I think over what he says, but it's so wrong I don't know how to begin to answer him. I try, "I'm sure even with the danger they would rather be free."

Norberto answers, "What do they know about being free? They're only birds. My father says freedom is overrated."

I cringe at this and dare to say, "What if a country has its liberty taken from it?"

"If you want to run a country properly, you sometimes have to sacrifice liberty to order."

His words are frightening. Eduardo, how can I beg him for your freedom if, to him, freedom means nothing?

Norberto picks up a pair of binoculars and inspects a large bird with a flute-like whistle in a thick fringe of tall reeds along the river's edge, its brown wings pumping slowly. "What is it?" I ask, afraid that right before my eyes some noose or net will snag the poor creature.

"Whistling heron. Do you want it?"

Horrified, I say, "No, no." How can I help but think of the prisoners Norberto's father has captured, of you, Eduardo, so that I have to clench my hands together to keep from hurrying from cage to cage to release the prisoners into the freedom of the sky?

A servant brings out a silver tray and I hear the clinking of ice in two tall glasses. There are silver straws to sip the lemonade and a plate of *alfajores*. As the woman leaves, she glances at the cages and shudders.

Norberto sits beside me and leaning over, kisses my throat.

I am not prepared and can't help turning aside. Hastily I whisper, "Your parents will see us."

He runs a hand along my bare arm. "They've got other things on their minds." In a hushed voice he says, "Father is afraid he is spending too much time here. He doesn't want the other generals to get the idea that for some reason he is hiding away, or there will be a grab for his job."

Here is an opportunity. "You sound as if you know a lot about your father's position."

"I know all about it," Norberto brags. "I hear him on the phone. And he talks to me. He wants to prepare me for a place in the government one day, so he tells me a lot about what's happening in the country. Papá is clever. When he sets his mind on something, no one is a match for him. This is confidential, but he has his eyes on General Videla's job. Last week he invited down here some of the generals who would support him against Videla. If Videla knew of Father's plans, he would have Father behind bars."

But I am not interested in the general's ambitions. I ask, "Would your father do something if you wanted him to?"

"Papá? Of course." He gives me a smug smile. "Why?"

"I just wondered." Norberto leans over and kisses me again. I manage not to cringe. He puts his arm around me and draws me close. His body is shivering like Dichoso's when a rabbit or a squirrel is close. I can't keep myself from jumping up. "I just don't feel comfortable doing that in your parents' home."

He grins at me. "Then we'll have to have a slow ride back in my car."

To escape him I wander over to the imprisoned birds. Norberto has taken up his binoculars and is looking across the river. I loosen the catch on the egret's cage. It has only to dance a bit and the cage door will open and the great bird will be free. I am amazed at what I have done. My courage is for you, Eduardo, and like the bird, I will set you free.

The maid returns to announce dinner. The four of us are lost sitting at the enormous table and I tremble under the general's attentive stare. Two servants wait upon us, one of them hovering over the general, who is eating a dinner of broth and chicken cut into small pieces. Our plates are heaped with a *bife de costilla,* the largest and most tender steak I have had since our day at Uncle Julio's ranch. Norberto's mother orders the servants to bring in more of this or that for us, as if we have just come from months of starvation. I think of you hungry and in prison, Eduardo, as I do every minute of the day, and my appetite disappears so that I can hardly put a forkful into my mouth.

The general notices. "I am forced to exist on little

morsels, but you can have what you like, young lady. I hope you are not letting some faddish diet tell you what you can eat. Women should have a little padding on them." He gives Norberto a knowing wink.

I am conscious of Señora López watching me during dinner. I think she guesses at my discomfort. As we get up from the table she says, "Norberto and his father can have one of their little chats while I show you the rest of the house." She leads me from one dark dispiriting room to another. The rooms look unlived in, as if this were a house of ghosts. Whenever she sees some little sign of life, a curtain pulled back, a sofa pillow crushed, an open book, she hastily straightens and clears away, removing any clue the place is inhabited by a family. When we come to what must be the general's study, she lingers at his desk, putting piles of paper into rigid order. She fingers a file and like a magician extracts a sheet of paper, which she tucks into her pocket. She has been so quick I am unsure of what I actually saw.

As we move into another room Señora López asks, "How long have you known my son?" Her voice is impersonal, but she is watching me closely.

"Only a short time," I say.

"Then you don't know him well." It is not a question. "You seem like a very nice young girl, one who has been well brought up. Norberto can be quite pleasant, but don't be deceived."

Her words unnerve me. "What do you mean?"

She finds a chair pulled out of place to catch the light from the window as if someone had been reading there. Hastily she returns it to its place. "This is an evil house," she says. "I have trouble keeping order here. Come, they'll be waiting for us."

Once again I doubt myself. I have counted on Norberto's tender feeling for me. Because he cares for me, Eduardo, he will care for you, but perhaps there is no tenderness, only a desire to possess me as he possesses his poor birds. "Don't be deceived," his mother said. If his mother does not trust him, how can I? I tell myself it is only an old woman's bitterness, that she is appalled at what her husband does and his influence on her son. I have seen hatred in the way she stares at the general, but there is no hatred when she looks at Norberto—only pity. It's not too late for me to abandon the whole scheme, to escape from Norberto and his malevolent father and disturbed mother. I know mine is a precarious plan. I know I might not succeed—but it is the only plan I have.

Later, when Norberto and I go out onto the terrace, Norberto asks, "What did you and Mamá talk about?"

I feel I must protect the señora. "Nothing. She was very nice."

"She is *loca,* crazy. She gives my father trouble all the time and one of these days he is going to have her put away."

Norberto suddenly stands still, staring. I look too. The door of the egret's cage is open. A thrill of pleasure and terror surges through me.

Norberto hurries over to see what has happened. I am afraid he will guess, but no, he only says, "I need to find better cages. The fool who made these doesn't know what he's doing. It's not a problem. I can easily get another egret next week."

Might General López free you, Eduardo, because it will be so easy to find another to take your place? I shudder at my thought. The general calls to us that he is ready to leave. I cast a glance at the row of cages and fight a compulsion to open all of them. Then I follow Norberto to the launch, dreading the moment we will be alone in the car.

As we prepare to board General López joins us. "I'll be driving back with you, son. I have an appointment tomorrow. Your mother pointed out that going along with you will save my driver a trip."

I see Norberto's face turn red with frustration and anger. "But, Papá, that's what you pay the driver for."

Color returns to his father's face. "I'll decide what I pay him for." It is the first harsh thing I have heard him say—all afternoon he has smiled fondly upon Norberto. Eduardo, is there a limit to what General López will do for his son?

Señora López says to Norberto, "I thought you would be pleased to have your father's company." A sly smile plays around her thin lips. Norberto gives her a killing look.

So it is settled that the general will go back in the car with us. I am so grateful that I could fling my arms around Señora López.

Eduardo

DEAR Silvia, I belong to General Remos. He wears thick glasses and if he tilts his head in a certain way, I see a reflection of myself. It terrifies me when that happens. I am afraid he has captured my soul so that I have become a part of him. Today he is kind, turning down the glaring light that blinds me and offering me a drink of water, something we are not allowed in our cells. He invites me to sit down, a great relief after hours of standing. He speaks kindly to me. "It is for your own sake that I urge you to answer my questions. If you cooperate I can assure you we will consider letting you go. You want your freedom back, don't you? You want to walk out of here and go back to your life? We are having a spell of fine weather," he says. "Only yesterday I took my son to the beach. Of course, he is much younger than you, but in some ways you remind me of him. Let me be a father to you. I want to help you to do what is best."

How can this man who has been torturing me speak of himself as my father? I think of my own father. I see what a worry I was to him demonstrating in front of the university, marching against the government, risking the charge of treason with my articles. What can he be feeling now? I don't regret my fight against the generals, but instead of being cautious so that I could go on to fight another day, I wanted everyone to see how courageous I was. Worst of all, my carelessness put my friends in danger.

Remos becomes confidential, sending the guard from the room and turning off the recorder. "Listen," he says, "you may not believe me, but in many things I am on your side. I don't approve of these tactics. There are some at the top who believe that to conquer, you must do evil. I don't believe that. I am waiting for the day when those who do are gone. I want to get rid of those in the government who delight in the prisons. You say you are for justice, so tell the truth. Trust me, I want to get rid of men like General López and his secret service. A man like myself," he says, "would know how to do a better job. There is no need to destroy the whole country to bring order to Argentina.

We are making an end of civil society in our hurry to punish, but I can do nothing until I find a way to get rid of those brutes who are in power now." He reaches in his desk and sensuously fingers a thick file as if it were something soft, a bit of velvet or a furry animal. Then he pushes the file back and closes the drawer with a snap.

I wonder why he is telling me this. I suppose it would be too dangerous for him to speak of such things to his fellow military men, but the thoughts are there and want to be let out. It is safe to tell me, for should I threaten to repeat his words, it would be nothing for him to destroy me. Or more likely it is a game, a means of ingratiating himself so that I trust him. But I do not. Like Professor Bustamante, my days of trusting are over. I am unsure I could trust *you,* Silvia.

"You must believe that this is not my doing," he says. "General López pushes us for results. Let me give him what he wants, and I will put in a good word for you. Believe me, I have no wish to continue this unpleasantness."

Remos doesn't know that I have had contact with Ramón. Ramón gave him what he wanted, and Ramón is still in prison. When I am silent he shakes his head sadly and calls the guards back. They put me on the table and bring the picana. He stalks out of the room. It is my time for prayer. I say all the prayers we learned as children, the prayers Mother made us say before we fell asleep, prayers to keep us safe in the dark.

Here even with the glare of the light in my eyes, there is only darkness.

I fall to the floor trembling and sobbing. Remos returns and says again that if only I will give the names of the rebels at the university and at the union, he will return me to Mother and Father. He tells me how Mother and Father are sick with worry about me. And he says, "You have a sister, Silvia, have you not? She will be a student at the university next year." How does he know your name?

When I get back to my cell Ramón taps a message, but I don't respond. I lay there. My fingers are burned beneath the nail and the pain is very bad. But that is not the worst of it. Suppose I told Ramón the truth? What if I tapped a message that said: "I am here because I would not murder your mother and sister"?

The Jackal had ordered me to continue to see Ramón's family. To gain time I followed his instruction. I went to the Fratelli home and told Señora Fratelli and Teresa, "I am here to help you.

With Ramón gone, let me be a son to you. Only tell me what I can do." I was a suitor, I brought them candies, *turrónes* stuffed with almonds and granizados sticky with caramel and rich with chocolate. I told myself that if I did not follow the Jackal's orders, someone else would.

"You are like Ramón," Señora Fratelli said, accepting my gifts. "He is such a considerate boy."

I said nothing to her against Ramón, but to myself I said, "*Considerate* is hardly the way to describe someone who not only gave his friends away, but went with the police to point them out."

Now I feel differently. There are moments during my torture when I would do the same. For me those moments pass, but there will come a time when they do not.

I spent time with Teresa, who could think only of her brother, as I believe you must think of me. Teresa was shy, like some small woodland creature that must be coaxed out of its lair. She let me accompany her one day to the Museo Nacional de Bellas Artes to see an exhibition of French paintings. "Ramón loved to paint," she said. "One day I'll show you some of his work. He had a wonderful eye for beauty."

I thought of Ramón shut up in his prison cell, with

nothing to see but the bare ugliness of cement walls and floors.

She stood in front of a painting by van Gogh, its slashes of greens and reds and blues like a child trying out color for the first time. "They say the artist was mad, that he spent time in an asylum. Still, when he left the place he painted this incredible picture, as if he were just waiting for the chance."

I knew she was hoping Ramón one day would emerge from his prison to begin painting again. I took her hand as we wandered in and out of the rooms looking at the canvases she said Ramón loved. "These paintings almost bring my brother back," she said.

Teresa's mother marched each afternoon at the Plaza de Mayo. Teresa would go and sit on a little bench nearby the circle of women, wanting to join in but too timid. She always held a book. I would sit beside her breathing in the faint lilac fragrance of the perfume she used. I wanted to put an arm around her and keep her safe, but I had to be satisfied with the warm touch of her hand as she shared her book to show me some poem that moved her. I thought in another time, a better time, Teresa and I would have had the whole city of Buenos Aires for our own, to wander in and discover as we learned to know each other. Now I was there not to care for Teresa but to destroy her.

"I know your mother's poems," she said. "Some of them by heart. She is a very brave woman. I wish I could write what I feel. I wish I could trap my heart and put it into words."

The only moments of peace I had were sitting there with Teresa in the park under the plane trees, trying to ignore what was going on around me. But one day she gathered up her confidence, and after kissing me, left me to join her mother and the other marching women.

A few days later the Jackal came to me. "The time has come. No more little tête-à-têtes with your Fratelli friends. Tomorrow I will give you the bomb. You will take it to their house. After a few minutes you will excuse yourself to use the bathroom. There you will arm the bomb, set it to go off in five minutes, and leave."

"They are innocent," I pleaded, "and brave. They march every afternoon in support of Ramón and all those who have disappeared. They had nothing to do with Ramón's betrayal. They are on our side." I tried to control my voice, but I longed to lunge at the Jackal, to throw him to the ground and choke the life from him.

He must have seen the hatred in my eyes. "I have

your articles in an envelope, safely hidden," he warned me. "If anything happens to me, they will go directly to the government."

The next day we met in a café in the Parque 3 de Febrero. There on a bench, surrounded by bloodred geraniums, he gave me the backpack in which he had concealed the bomb. The instructions on how to arm it were so simple, I thought it a wonder the world was still here. Before I could say anything, he was gone.

You remember, Silvia, how as little children we tagged along with Mother when she shopped? We were bored and would pass the time by playing at hiding from each other. This time it was not a game. I entered buildings and left by their back entrances. I stood at a shop window and watched the reflections of those who passed to see if someone was following me. I ran through alleys and up and down stairs, all the while aware of the bomb in my backpack, wondering if something would accidentally set it off. At last I believed I had escaped the Jackal's surveillance. I made my way to the river. I put a chunk of concrete into the backpack and watched it sink into the water.

At the Fratelli home, the señora welcomed me. "Eduardo, I have just made a pot of gnocchi. It was Ramón's favorite dish and when I make it I dream of him hurrying into the kitchen and throwing his arms around me, pleased at the treat to come. When I heard the bell, I thought, Perhaps he knew, perhaps he has come back to us." She wiped away tears and urged me to share their meal. "Teresa will be so pleased to see you."

Teresa gave me an open smile and took my hand. Marching each day had given her courage, and now she was less shy with me. "Eduardo, you look like you're in a great hurry. Can't you sit down and join us for dinner?"

"There's no time for dinner. For the three of us there is no time at all." I was aware of the savagery of my words, but I had to convince them of the danger. "Listen to me. I was ordered to deliver a bomb to your home."

They stared at me as if I had suddenly become deranged. Señora Fratelli appeared ready to run. She grabbed Teresa.

Hastily I said, "I threw the bomb into the river. It was meant to be punishment for Ramón. They say he gave names away during his imprisonment."

Teresa said, "You mean he caused others to be arrested? My brother would never do that."

"You must understand he was under great stress,

but some on our side haven't forgiven him. It was my job to kill the two of you as a warning to others of what would happen to their families if they gave information."

Señora Fratelli stared at me. "Kill *us*?"

"Yes. Now others will come who will do what I would not. You must leave Argentina at once."

With tears in her eyes, Teresa asked, "What will happen to you? You haven't carried out their orders."

"It doesn't matter. I will leave home as well."

Señora Fratelli insisted, "I will never leave Argentina while Ramón is in prison."

"You may be willing to die," I said, "but what of Teresa? She will die too."

Señora Fratelli recoiled as if I had struck her.

"For that's what will happen," I said. "Neither of you are safe. You must go at once. Take nothing. Just walk out of the back door, as I will do. And never return."

Señora Fratelli looked around frantically, but she was not thinking of her possessions. Crazily she said, "The gnocchi are cooking."

"Mamá," Teresa said. "You go and turn the stove off. I know where you keep the emergency money and I'll get your medicine."

In a minute they were back. Señora Fratelli scooped

up a picture of Ramón. She embraced me. Teresa took my hand and brought it to her lips. After I heard the door close I gave them as long a time as I dared, then followed them to the world outside—a world that I would soon lose.

I had planned to get Father by himself that night and tell him what I had been doing, wondering what he would think when he heard me say words like *prison* and *bombs*. Then the police came and it was too late. The Jackal must have predicted my betrayal; he must have turned over my articles even before I left for the Fratellis'.

Remos is reading those articles to me, ridiculing a sentence here and there. He tosses the articles onto the table and dismisses them.

A guard reaches for the picana.

I begin to think of people I can betray. Who will I send to prison? César? María? Why, Silvia, did Remos mention your name?

Silvia

DEAREST Eduardo, time is running out. Only today Rosa's older sister, Alicia, and her husband, Manuel, were sitting in a café and the police came in demanding everyone's papers. They took Manuel away. Rosa's family are terrified—no one could be more innocent than Manuel, who is so caught up with his research he hardly knows who General Videla is. There are more executions. They say the prisons are overcrowded and they must make room.

I try to tell myself my plan is working. Norberto is attentive and always there. Isabela came to me today to plead with me to stop seeing him. "He makes my flesh creep," Isabela said. "What can you be thinking? You don't have any friends left. How can you be seen with Norberto López when your own brother is suffering in prison and it was Norberto's father who sent him there? Silvia, I know you. You're not a fool. What's going on?"

I had to let someone know. I needed someone to stand with me. I have known Isabela since kindergarten and was sure I could trust her. It was to Isabela that I confided in fifth grade the name of the boy I liked, and as a freshman my crush on my Spanish teacher. She never gave me away. While I dash at things, Isabela turns everything around and around. I took hold of her hand. "Do you absolutely promise not to say anything?"

"Yes, of course."

Before I had even finished my story she interrupted me. "Silvia, you can't do this! It's too dangerous. You can't trust Norberto López. He's a snake."

My plan was all I had. I couldn't let her discourage me. "How can you say that? You don't know him. He really likes me, and I know I can make him help Eduardo."

"That's the trouble with you, Silvia. You think everyone is good. What if he turns against you? What will happen to you then?"

"I don't care. It's the only way to save my brother."

After that, whenever I saw Isabela she gave me a troubled look and I knew she wanted to stop me, but she kept her promise and said nothing. Rosa didn't know of my plan and would merely look away, refusing even to acknowledge me.

The painful part was deceiving Mother and Father, for now Norberto came to our house to call for me and to bring me home.

At first, Father had no idea Norberto was related to General López, but a friend must have warned him. He and Mother were waiting for me one evening when I had been out with Norberto.

"Silvia," Father said solemnly, "come into my study. Your mother and I want to talk with you."

You will remember, dear Eduardo, how when Father summoned us into his study we knew we had done something wrong? I guessed what was coming.

Mother put her hand on mine. "Silvia, we have never interfered with your friends. We always depend on your good sense, but we must tell you who Norberto's father is. You cannot know, or you would never have gone out with him. His father, General López, is the head of the secret service." Mother and Father waited for me to express my shock.

Instead, I said, "You have always told me to judge a person for himself, not to judge him by his family."

"Yes. Yes, of course," Father said. "But General

López is responsible for the arrests and disappearances, the murders in many cases, of perfectly innocent people! Norberto knows what his father does."

Mother said, "We have reason to believe that General López gave the order for your brother's arrest. You cannot possibly want to carry on a relationship with his son."

"He's not like his father," I said. "He can be very nice."

Mother stared at me aghast. "You mean you knew? Oh, Silvia, have you forgotten your brother?" Tears filled her eyes. I reached for her hand but she drew it away.

Father said, "There is something else, something which you must not repeat, especially to Norberto. General López is a patient of mine. It is enough that I must treat the vicious man, it is unthinkable that you should have anything to do with him or his family."

Mother turned on Father. "Do you meant to say you agreed to treat a man like that?"

"He is very ill and needs an operation to save his life. That operation happens to be my specialty. He insists that I be the one to do it. And there are special arrangements that must be made regarding his privacy. Adela, I can barely stand being in the same room with that man, but I am a doctor. A doctor, like a priest, is obliged to give help *wherever* it is needed."

Mother insisted, "Surely you can make some excuse!"

"No. I must operate and let us hope the outcome is successful." He paused as if he had been about to say something more.

"Successful!" Mother said. "It would be a mercy to the country if he should die."

"You have no idea what you are saying, Adela. You must know that there are more General Lópezes waiting in line." Father turned to me. "I may be obliged to treat the father, but you are not obliged to date the son. I thought I would never do this, Silvia, but I forbid you to see that boy. If you can't understand what is at stake, I must make the decision for you."

I was stung by Father's anger but, Eduardo, I still don't dare tell Mother and Father my plan. They would see only the danger and none of the hope. And as long as Norberto cares for me, I believe there is hope. I have begun to meet Norberto at the disco, telling him, "You know how parents are. They think I'm too young to see one boy so often."

So I am alone now.

◆ ◆ ◆

Eduardo, if you are to be saved I must go very soon to Norberto with my plea. More bodies have been discovered in the river. It is rumored the victims were dropped from helicopters while still alive. I live in terror that one of those bodies is yours.

Today I have my chance. It is a warm afternoon, the sun making light and dark just where it wishes. Norberto chooses an outdoor café for our lunch. We sit under the trees sipping iced tea. Norberto says, "I want to show you my parents' apartment. This is confidential, but Papá is seeing some doctor who wants him in the hospital today for tests, and Mamá is still at Tigre. We'll have the apartment all to ourselves."

It is the perfect opportunity. I know the risks. I know what Isabela and Mother and Father would say, but each day, Eduardo, brings you closer to death. You would say you'd prefer to die rather than have me sacrifice my safety, but it is not your decision. You will never learn what I am going to do. You will only taste freedom.

Norberto runs his hand gently up my bare arm. He smiles at me. He is thinking about the apartment. I tell Norberto, "Yes, I'd love to see your home." Alone with him, where no one can see us, I will pour out my heart. I will plead with him to ask his father to let you go. I am more frightened than I have ever been in my life, but I console myself with the thought that soon you and I will be together and you will be free. *Free.*

On the way to the López apartment we drive past my school. I think of my history class with its tedious lectures and how I had hated sitting through them. Now I would give anything in the world to be walking into the simple world of that classroom. Norberto drives with one arm, his other arm around my shoulder holding me tightly. I think of all the birds at Tigre. "Did you find another great egret?" I ask.

"Yes, and that whistling heron as well. I had new cages built. No danger of their getting away now."

The López apartment is in the Palarmo section of the city, in a mansion that has been sectioned into four apartments. There is a guard at the entrance who evaluates me. I feel I am something in a store showcase. He looks away, deciding I am just one more of Norberto's girls—and what if I am? Norberto opens the apartment door and gives me a little push inside as if I were a reluctant child. I can't find the proper words and play for time. I ask Norberto to show me the apartment. The tour he gives me is hurried, as if I were a prospective buyer and he did not want to sell. The fine moldings and fireplaces and the floor-length windows that open onto balconies all tell of an earlier time when a noble family occupied the house. The apartment, like the mansion in Tigre, is immaculate, and I have a hard time believing people actually live there. Señora López has worked hard to scrub away the sinister presence of the general from the rooms.

Norberto ends the tour in his bedroom. It is decorated with pennants from World Cup matches. There is a photograph of Norberto as a small boy with the famous fútbol star Pelé, and on Norberto's dresser a large bronze trophy inscribed with his name and the name of his junior team. There are clothes hung over the chair backs and records piled up in a slipshod way on the floor. When I look surprised, Norberto says, "I don't allow my mother in my room."

I shiver. Without the exorcism of his mother's tidying, wickedness remains in the room. Still, there is something of the schoolboy in the trophies and the fútbol souvenirs. I imagine Norberto as a youngster coming home from school, his knees skinned from practice, his shirt pulled out, pleased with himself for making the winning goal. It is to that schoolboy that I appeal. "Norberto, being around your father, you must hear what is going on in the city. There is talk of more arrests and even more executions."

Norberto shrugs. "I don't listen to talk like that. The government does what it must. Why should we tolerate fools who want to destroy this country? As far as I'm concerned the time for mercy is over."

He picks out a record from the disorderly pile and puts it on. He begins to dance and reaches out for me. I force a smile and follow his steps, but the next moment he pushes me onto his bed. The surprise is so great that without thinking of what I have set out to do, I spring away from his grasp.

"You're not going to be coy, are you?"

I know that there is no more time. I take a deep breath. "Please listen to me, Norberto. I need to ask you to do something, something that means everything to me."

He is still lying on the bed. He looks up at me, a flinty smile on his face. "What do you mean?"

"Norberto, you have to help me. I haven't told you, but my brother, Eduardo, is in prison. You said if you asked your father for a favor he would give it. If you care for me, promise me you will ask the general to free my brother."

Norberto gets up from the bed and stands looking at me. "Do you think I don't know who you are? That your father is Doctor Díaz, who is treating my father, and that your foolish brother has been arrested? Do you think my father did not investigate you? After I took you to Tigre he asked questions about you. When he found out who you were, he wanted me to stop seeing you, but I told him I could deal with you, and do you know what he said? 'Take what you want but don't get too serious, son. That is not a family we want to associate with.'"

I feel as if I have been thrown into an icy river. Why didn't I realize General López would know all there was to know about any girl his son brought to his home? How can I have been so naive? Still I refuse to give up. "Please, Norberto, I've seen how you love the birds. You have a heart."

"I love the softness of the birds. That is what I love about you, Silvia, your softness. You aren't hard like the other girls. You are soft." He grasps my arm and squeezes it until I cry out.

"Your brother is alive for now. A word from me and he will be dead. I won't free your brother, but you will do what I want or I'll have him eliminated. You're right—my father does listen to me."

Everything has changed. I am furious with myself and with Norberto, but I won't let the general and his son win. Norberto starts to pull me onto the bed.

I break away. When he comes after me I reach for the bronze trophy and slam it against his head. He stares, unbelieving, and then falls onto the bed. Blood starts to trickle from a cut on his forehead.

The door opens. Has the general somehow found out what I have done and come to arrest me for murder? It is Norberto's mother. After a brief glance at me she runs to the bed and cradles her son's head in her hands, covering him with kisses.

"Is he dead? Did I kill him?"

"No, no. He is coming around, but you must leave at once. There will be no holding Norberto back when he sees you. I know my son. He will call his father."

"General López put my brother in prison. I only wanted to ask Norberto to help free him. I never meant to hurt your son." I sink down onto a chair and cover my eyes with my hands to shut out everything in the room.

"It's my fault," Señora López says. "I knew you were not a girl to love a boy like my son. I make it my business to know what my husband knows, so I knew that your brother is a guest in one of my husband's prisons. I guessed that you thought Norberto could be of help to him. You are a very foolish girl to think that you could outwit my son. He has his father and the whole army behind him."

"What brought you here?"

"I was concerned for you. I learned Norberto had dismissed the servants at the apartment for the day. I suspected he was bringing you here." While she talks, Señora López caresses Norberto, bending down from time to time to kiss him.

"What should I do?" I ask. "Your husband will have my brother killed. He will send the soldiers after me and my family."

"Not your family. Your father is to operate on my husband tomorrow. He will preserve your father, at least until the operation is over, but I fear for you and for your brother. My husband worships his son, and Norberto will be furious. You must leave at once and stay away from your family. Their home will be the first place they look. Make no mistake. I love my son, but it's because I love him that I wanted to stop him from doing something despicable. It's enough that his father should do evil things."

Norberto opens his eyes, looks blankly about, and closes them again. Has he seen me? I am terrified and can't move. Señora López gets up from the bed and puts a hand on my shoulder, pushing me roughly toward the door. "Leave at once." She thrusts a large envelope at me. "I have brought you a gift. The time has come for the terror to stop. Take this with you and give it to your father. It may save all of you."

Instead of your freedom, I hold an envelope in my hand. It means nothing to me—the señora must be mad. I can't spend one more moment in this apartment. I want to breathe fresh air. Then I realize what I have done and what will happen to me, and I know I cannot escape.

The señora tightens her hand on my shoulder. "Tell your father to operate and make my husband well. I would not want him to escape his years in jail. I might have forgiven him for what he has done to the country, but I will not forgive him for corrupting my son. Now go!" She turns toward Norberto, whose eyes are opening again. This time they are focusing, first on his mother and then on me.

If before I had seen desire for me, there is no desire in his eyes now, only rage and revenge.

Eduardo

MY dear Silvia, Ramón isn't responding to my taps. That is not unusual, for he has been spending longer and longer hours in interrogation. I suffer now for the two of us, and the burden is heavy. I no longer believe in the lies I tell myself about the torture ending. I won't hold out. I'll tell what I know. My only comfort is to think of Teresa and her mother away from Argentina and safe. Teresa once told me they had relatives in Uruguay—I imagine they took the ferry across the Plata River to Montevideo. I remember in another lifetime how our student fútbol team went to Montevideo for a match. We celebrated our win in the cafés along the Rambla, the wide boulevard that follows the river. I see Teresa, there, walking with no fear, looking across the river to Buenos Aires. I believe Teresa and Señora Fratelli will stay in Montevideo, close to Buenos Aires, hoping that one day Ramón will be freed to take up his brush and paint. Then I shudder as I think of the pictures their Ramón might paint now, pictures of what his life has become.

Ramón does not return to his cell. I hear a helicopter lift off from the prison yard. The helicopters fly over the Plata River or the Paraná River or over the wide sea to drop their human cargo into the mute waters. I have heard the tales of how they are sometimes careless and do not use enough cement to anchor the bodies to the ocean floor, so that the corpses wash up onto the shore.

I consider where I wish my body thrown. Into the sea, I decide. Somewhere where endless water will wash away all of this misery. It is terrible being without Ramón. Our jailers must know how much strength and courage the small touch of another human life gives, for I will suffer twice as much when I have only my own poor, dwindling bit of courage.

This is the longest night of my life. I go over the past, turning over the pages of my years, searching for something that for even a few moments will lift me out of this hell and the certain knowledge of tomorrow's pain. I look for a memory strong enough.

I try the bright summer's day when Mother and Father took us to Mar del Plata for the weekend. We had been invited to stay with friends who had an apartment at the resort by the sea. You and I were allowed to go by ourselves to the beach. I was twelve, embarrassed at having to watch over a little sister. You could hardly see the sand for the crowds on the beach. Every chair had its brightly colored umbrella. The whole seaside was filled with yellow circles like so many small suns. You claimed a square of sand and began to build a castle, decorating it with bits of shell and sea glass. When I offered to help, you pushed me away. You were always independent. You always knew what you wanted and went after it.

I left you building your castle and ran into the water, pitying the timid children who were standing uncertain and shivering in the shallow water. I had once been afraid of the water, and Father, embarrassed by my fear, was going to throw me into the deep end of the pool, thinking to cure my fear by more fear. You saved me by distracting him. Little as you were, Silvia, you were brave enough to paddle into the deep end when I couldn't. Because of your example I set about learning to swim well.

That day in Mar del Plata I waded past the people and out to where the river was deep. I plunged into the water. There were few swimmers that far out and

I had the river to myself. When I came up for a breath I turned my head away from the shore and saw only the river that flowed into the sea. I had no fear. The water was not an enemy but a friend, holding me safely in its arms.

I had left you playing on the beach knowing you had been the one to send me into the freedom of the deep water. You not only made me a fine swimmer, but you helped me find a strength I didn't know I had. Though you could not understand my motives, without that courage from you I would not have taken up the fight against the generals and their repression and murders.

Alone here in my cell I worry that my arrest will lead you into a desperate act to help me. I worry that you will risk your life as you did in the pool when I hadn't the courage to plunge in. I want to believe you are safely on the shore, as you were that day at Mar del Plata, far away from the danger that I swim in every second of the day. But I know you too well. Worry about what the generals might do to those of us who protested made you want to hide in the spending of your time with clothes and dancing, but that was never the real Silvia. I tremble to think what the real Silvia will do to save me this time. I tell myself it would be for the best if I made them finish me off so you would not attempt something foolish. Then I tell myself that if I were to give in, you would never forgive me.

I have these conversations in my head. I say one thing, and then another me tells me something else, and the two parts never agree. Each one can argue convincingly.

The guard comes to take me to General Remos. Today he is playing the roll of a schoolmaster, wanting to argue me out of my beliefs. "You must admit this country was in chaos," he says. "Bombings on both sides. The guerrillas kidnapping innocent people and holding them for ransom to buy guns to destroy our country. Something had to be done. The military only wished to establish order." He says this in a forced voice, as if he is trying to convince himself. "If a few innocent people are sacrificed, that's a small price to pay."

I stand in front of his desk for what seems hours, and I am so tired I can barely express myself, but I must answer him. "You believe innocent people like myself and my friends can be sacrificed for the good of the state because you place no value on us. You believe the state is more important than the individual. I believe just the opposite. The state exists to protect the individual."

"That is the kind of foolishness you put in your articles. You are a gullible boy." With the tip of his pen Remos nudges the familiar folder of my articles as if it were unclean. "You must know who sent us your articles, who betrayed you. Why not give us his name?"

"His betrayal would be no excuse for my doing the same. Anyhow, it wouldn't do you any good. He will have long since disappeared and be hiding under another name and another identity."

"Your articles criticizing the government are the work of a child."

I goad him. "Then why do you keep mentioning them?"

He stands up and slaps my face. I am weak with standing so long, and the strength of the blow knocks me to my knees. After hours under the glaring lights, the cement floor feels cool under my hands. Beneath the desk I see Remos's shiny boots. I watch, helpless, as one of the boots comes at me. I feel a sharp pain in the side of my head.

The guard is called and I am dragged away to my cell. I resolve that when next I see him I will say whatever Remos wants, but then a small thing happens. It is odd that while we wait for the grand events that will make a difference, one small thing can change our lives.

Somewhere in the blocks of concrete there must exist a tiny opening, a tunnel leading from the world on the outside to my cell, for a mouse has found its way to me, a brown mouse with a white chest and four white paws. He has jet bead eyes and busy whiskers. The insides of his ears are pink rose petals. I am rigid with stillness, for the presence of even so small a living creature is comforting. He discovers a crumb on the floor, thrusts it into his mouth, and scampers about searching for more crumbs. When nothing is to be found he sits on his haunches and proceeds to clean his whiskers. All the life in the world seems packed into that scrap of animal, as if the mouse might explode with life. I am not alone. Whatever happens to me doesn't matter, for the world has millions and millions of small creatures who are not timid. Together we are stronger than all the generals.

Silvia

SEÑORA López warned me not to go home, but, Eduardo, where else can I go? I'll throw together a few clothes, find some money, and then like all the others before me, I will disappear. If Norberto catches me, he will cage me like one of his birds. I'd rather die.

When I reach home I'm relieved to find Mother and Father arguing. With all their attention on the quarrel, they don't notice how upset I am. I make for the stairway and my suitcase, but when I hear the general's name I cannot move.

Father is saying, "Adela, you must understand why I am fighting so hard to save General López's life and to keep his illness a secret. There are generals out there who are after López's position. They would like nothing better than to discover that he is ill and vulnerable. They would pounce. I have had to make elaborate arrangements at the hospital to preserve his privacy. No one will know on whom I am operating. In exchange, the general has agreed to my conditions. He believes not only his life but his position in the government depends on agreeing to paying my price."

"What do you mean 'paying your price'?" Mother asks. "I don't understand. You have performed operations for nothing for people who can't afford them, and he is a rich man."

Without thinking I say, "That's true. The López place in Tigre must be worth a fortune."

They both stare at me. Father says, "You have been to Tigre?"

I have given myself away. I mustn't involve my parents in what I have done. Hastily I say, "Just the once. I wasn't alone with Norberto. His mother and father were there."

Father's face is white. "I forbade you to see Norberto, and not only did you disobey me, I now learn you have been in the same house with General López."

"The visit to Tigre was before you told me not to see Norberto."

"The general must know you are my daughter." Father is looking at me in a strange way.

I can't keep the truth from my face.

All this time Mother is studying me as she studies the work of some poet whose obscure words hold a deep and secret meaning. At last she puts her arms around me. "Silvia, tell us what happened."

In her arms, I can't hold back. The whole story tumbles out. "It was only to save Eduardo. I am sure they will come after me now. I have to get away."

Father is crying. I have never seen him cry, even when they took you, Eduardo. "Oh, Silvia," he says. "All that was unnecessary. My price to operate was always Eduardo's release. López promised that he would find a way of quietly letting Eduardo go. What will he do now when he finds out what you have done to his son? Now López has two sticks to beat us with."

Eduardo, everything I did for you was for nothing.

"Don't scold Silvia," Mother begs. "It was a very foolish but a brave thing she did. I am so grateful to the general's wife. She saved you."

I am still clutching the useless envelope Señora López had given me and now, anxious to get rid of anything that has to do with the López family, I thrust it at Father. "Señora López said to give this to you."

Father pays no attention to the envelope, throwing it onto his desk. "You have only minutes to escape." He reaches into his pocket and empties his wallet. Mother flies about gathering more money and I stuff some clothes into a bag.

"Memorize this address," Father says. His hands are trembling. "I don't dare drive you. They'll be looking for my car. Take a taxi to the middle of the city and then a bus so they can't trace the taxi all the way. I know the people at this address, and they will help you get out of the country."

So Father has his secrets too.

I throw my arms around Mother and Father, saying my good-byes, the tears on our faces mingling. But when I open the door a policemen stands there, his hand raised, ready to knock. Behind him are four other policemen. They grab my shoulders, hustle me away, and throw me into a van. I am blindfolded and pushed onto the floor. Eduardo, is this how they took you away?

Perhaps they will exchange me for you, perhaps after all I have found a way to free you. I am terrified of torture or death, but I will endure it if they will let you go. But what if Father is right? Unless he does what they ask, not only you, Eduardo, but I too am at the mercy of López. Father will have to operate on General López and on anyone else the generals wish. I can scarcely breathe. As the van speeds along I pray for some fatal accident that will save my life by destroying it.

I am led blindfolded, my wrists and ankles in shackles, down a long corridor. I stumble several times until I learn to manage the shackles by a lurching side-to-side movement. I am pushed into a room where my blindfold is removed. A military officer sits at a desk staring at me, a quizzical look on his face. He is the one who will carry out General López's orders. This is the man who will have the power of life and death over me. He says, "I did not expect to see someone so young and so attractive. What can a girl like you have done to infuriate the López family?"

I am afraid that every word I say may incriminate me—or worse, you, Eduardo. When I remain silent he says, "It is very unusual to have the general make a direct request." The tone of his voice as he speaks of "the general" and "the López family" is impatient, even a little bitter. What if he doesn't like doing their business? Perhaps he will welcome anything bad I say about the general. He might not treat me so harshly if I give him information against López. But what if anything I say about General López is passed on to the general himself? Then it would go very badly for me and for you, Eduardo. But I have nothing else to bargain with.

"What do you know of General López?" he asks.

I remember how Father has said that General López wanted to keep his illness a secret and I say, "I almost feel sorry for the general. He can't be responsible for what he does."

Alert, the man demands, "What do you mean?"

"Since he is so sick. He is not like himself."

The man's eyes widen and he licks his lips. I have his attention. "You know of such an illness? Of course there have been rumors."

He leans toward me and I guess I am right to think he wants to know more about the general. "He has a very serious condition," I say. "My father is going to operate on him tomorrow."

He studies my file and must see that Father is a physician. He listens closely as I describe my visit to Tigre and the general's weakness. "He had trouble walking and he looked very ill."

"And this operation? It will cure him?"

"I don't know."

"Your father has done such operations in the past?"

"Yes, many."

"And his patients survived?"

I could have lied, but Father has written several papers about his good results. "Yes," I admit.

"Well then." There is a look of disappointment on his face. "If anyone can survive, it would be General López. You had better prepare yourself for a long stay."

All this time I have been thinking of you, Eduardo, wondering if you were dead or if by some miracle you were still alive. I can't help asking, "Is my brother here?" I think I can stand anything if you are nearby.

For an answer he asks, "What kind of mother and father do you have to raise such foolish children? Perhaps things will go easier for you and your brother if you give us information about your parents. If we learn, for example, that they have spoken against the generals, we might make it easier for you. We will say you were young and easily influenced by what you heard at home."

Hastily I declare, "My parents don't care about politics. They never spoke to us of politics." It was true. Until you were arrested, Eduardo, Father would have nothing to do with what was going on in the country.

He cared only for his profession. Mother did not care about politics either; she wrote her poems about the suffering of others. That was truth and not politics. Now truth has disappeared just as we have.

The man does not like my answer. "After you have been here a while I believe you will remember the words your parents spoke that turned the two of you into rebels." He motions to the guard to take me away. As I follow the guard, the steel clamps rub against my wrists and ankles. I stare at each cell door wondering, Eduardo, if one of the cells might be yours. How I long to beat on the doors and shout out your name; instead I have to stumble silent and frightened, until I am pushed roughly into a cell and the door is bolted.

Eduardo, you must be in a cell like mine. Apart from an iron cot, there is nothing in the room, no sign of the others who have occupied it. I don't want to think what has happened to them or what will happen to me. I know that if I can prepare myself, I will be less frightened of what comes, but everything from the stories of torture to the tales of bodies washed up along the river do nothing but paralyze me. With such stories, how is it possible to continue to hope?

There is a kind of scraping or tapping on the wall, so I know another prisoner is in the adjoining cell.

There seems to be a pattern to the tapping, but I can't make it out. I tap on the wall in answer, to let him know he is not alone.

I sit on the cot rubbing my wrists where the shackles have chafed them. The glare of the single electric bulb is like a malevolent eye staring at me. My thoughts are all I have for company, and try as I will, I can't escape them. All my efforts have led to this, and where will this lead? The hope I had of freeing you has vanished. I have no idea of time, which once seemed a gift but now is a punishment. An hour or two hours pass. My door opens and a guard pushes in a tray. On the tray is a bowl of watery soup and a scrap of bread. The food means nothing to me. I can't imagine ever eating again. The man stands there staring at me. With his broad shoulders and large hands, he is a man meant to guard others. His uniform is freshly pressed and I picture him each morning putting it on with pride. The way he studies me makes me nervous. I curl up and retreat onto a corner of my cot.

"You look like the boy," he says.

"What boy?" I am shaking

"The boy in there." He inclines his head to the next cell.

"What's his name?" I ask. I hold my breath.

He shakes his head and starts to shut the door.

"Wait," I cry. "Wait. Is it Eduardo Díaz? Please, is it my brother?"

He does not look like a kind man. How could he be and come here day after day in his freshly pressed uniform and listen to cries for mercy?

"Prisoners have no names."

"Can you at least tell me how he is?" I have stopped breathing.

The guard surveys me and then answers, "He survives."

I think the guard must be an angel sent to walk through these corridors and give bits and pieces of hope like drops of water for those dying of thirst. I don't know if it is you, Eduardo, but when the guard leaves I put my hands on the wall that separates me from the nameless prisoner. If desire were strength, the wall would fall to pieces.

Eduardo

THE guard comes for me. I have no more strength. I will tell Remos whatever I know. When I am shoved into the room I see Remos is speaking on the phone. He is holding the phone as if it were a small rabid animal. "Yes, General López," he says. "Yes, if that is what you want. Of course. I understand." He has the desk drawer open again and with his free hand is fingering the file as he always does when he is angry. He slams down the receiver.

In a voice heavy with sarcasm he says, "It appears General López is after all a merciful man. He has ordered me to let you go in exchange for another prisoner. You have only to agree."

What can he mean? I feel a little shiver of hope, so unaccustomed I hardly recognize it. But who is this prisoner? What must I agree to?

The door opens. The other prisoner. I turn to look expecting to see Ramón. It is not Ramón. I can't breathe. I have no voice.

It is you, Silvia. What have you done?

Then I remember what Remos has said. I may be exchanged for another prisoner. Go free while you remain? I would die first.

Before I can move Remos warns, "You are not to make any communication with each other, either by speech or physical contact. If you disobey there will be punishment for both of you."

He does not forbid our looking at each other. I can see in the shocked expression on your face, Silvia, a mirror of how I must look to you. Tears run down your cheeks. You are holding your hands out in front of you. I see the handcuffs have chaffed your slim wrists, leaving ugly welts. Before I can think what I am doing, I say to Remos, "Please take her handcuffs off."

He gives me a furious look. Then, as if he has had second thoughts, he nods at the guard, who removes them. Remos says to you, "Tell me more about this operation your father is going to do on General López."

At once I am alert. What operation is this? I give you a warning glance. You think you can make friends with Remos. You are eager to tell Remos anything he wants to hear. You do not know him. I try with my eyes to signal you to say nothing.

"Father was going to make special arrangements so that no one would know about the general's illness and the operation."

Remos is attentive. He pulls the file from his desk and tells the guard to leave. As soon as the guard is gone, Remos says, "Ah, special arrangements. That accounts for it." He sighs and makes some notes in his file. He straightens his shoulders as if he is bringing himself to attention. As if he is preparing himself for some task he wishes he could avoid but that he will carry out because it is his duty. At last he says, "That is why General López has ordered me to free one of you."

I can see, Silvia, that you are excited, even hopeful, but you have not been where I have been and experienced what I have. I wait.

"General López will free one of you. He has ordered me to tell you that which one must be your choice."

I say, "Silvia."

At the same moment you say, "Eduardo."

"Let me make myself plain," Remos says. "The one

who remains, remains a prisoner." He turns to you, Silvia. "Your brother could tell you what that is like, and let me assure you, things will go no easier for you because you are a girl. Perhaps one of you will wish to reconsider."

"Silvia, listen to me," I plead, "I have survived and I will survive. You must take this chance for freedom."

Though it is against the rule, Remos has let us speak to each other. He listens. He must hope we will give something away.

You say, "If only I had not been such a fool, Eduardo, Father would have been able to save you. What has happened is all my doing. I nearly killed General López's son when all I wanted was to find a way to free you. It's all my fault. General López is furious with me. He wants to punish both of us."

Remos sits up in his chair. For a moment he seems to forget that we are there. He says, "The general has carried out his own agenda in your arrests. That is not what an honorable soldier does. Our battle must not be about petty personal squabbles." Surreptitiously I see him reach for his file and make some notes. As he replaces the file he tests its thickness.

He says, "I can't say that I will be able to help you, but the more information I have, the more just a decision I can make." He turns to you, Silvia. "Tell me exactly what happened."

I'm afraid. I know this man. I have to speak. "Don't say anything, Silvia, it's just a trick to get you into more trouble."

"But you must already know," you say to him, "or I wouldn't be here."

"I will tell you something," Remos says. "General López is not a favorite of mine. There are some who believe that López is destroying the honor and tradition of the military with his secret vendettas. There are men who could do his job as it should be done. Men who would restore honor and integrity to the military." I see from his greedy look that Remos believes he is such a man. That is why he makes notes on the general—he wants to destroy López. All these months he has been silently nourishing his hatred; now he cannot stop himself from speaking out.

Remos asks you, "How did you come to meet the general's son?"

You hesitate and then in a small voice, you say, "I thought if I became friendly enough with General López's son, he would get his father to let Eduardo go."

"How friendly?"

You blush. I want to leap across the desk and strangle the breath from Remos. I try to move but I am weak and my leg irons make me stumble.

He sees my rage. He knows I will lose control and then you might stop answering his questions. Quickly he changes the subject and asks you, "Did you ever meet General López himself?"

"Oh, yes, I went with Norberto, that's the general's son, to their summer home in Tigre."

"Ah, yes," Remos says. "I know about the vacation home in Tigre. I wouldn't mind having a place in Tigre myself." He nudges the file and I see that he thinks if he could get rid of López he might one day have what López has. "What happened in Tigre?" he asks.

"I met the general and his wife. She hates him."

Remos pounces. "How do you know that?"

"She told me." You pause as if you have remembered something. I don't know where all of this is leading, and I fear what is coming.

"Yes?" Remos encourages you.

"When I left their apartment in Palarmo, Norberto's mother gave me an envelope. I think there were things in it that belonged to General López. She was angry with the general for the way he was raising Norberto. She said the envelope might save us."

Remos's face goes white and then red. "Where is this envelope now?"

You say, "I left it with my parents. I gave it to them when the police came to take me away."

Remos stands up. He says, "We are going to your house. But make no mistake—if what you tell me is true, if such an envelope exists, all may be well for you, for both of you. But if you are not telling me the truth . . . before I free one of you, both of you will find out how I treat liars."

He calls the guard and tells him to put your handcuffs back on. Then he gives an order for a car to be brought around. When the guard looks puzzled at the order, Remos shouts at him to hurry. You are placed in the backseat next to Remos and I am in the front seat next to the driver. As we take our places, I manage to brush your arm. The touch gives me a stillness and a feeling that is almost like hope. Then I hear Remos give our address and it terrifies me. I don't want Remos's devilry anywhere near our home.

As we drive through the city I am amazed that everything is as it was. How can that be? How has the world still gone on? The car pulls up and I see Remos study our house, a comfortable middle-class home. He says, "You had everything you could want.

Why weren't you content with your lives? Why did you have to meddle in affairs that had nothing to do with you? What is it to you what happens to traitors you don't know?" He tells the driver to wait in the car and prods us up the steps in front of him.

Remos pounds on the door. Father opens it. Mother is beside him. She places her hand over her mouth to keep from crying out. They reach for us, but Remos threatens us with his gun. He forces his way into the house, shoving us ahead of him.

"All of you, stay quiet. I haven't come to arrest you," he assures them. "Just listen and ask no questions. Your lives and the lives of your children will depend on what you tell me. You have an envelope that might have information on General López."

Father is unsure. After a moment he says, "I don't know what you mean. We have no such envelope."

"Your daughter told me you have the envelope. Are you saying she lied?"

"We had it," Mother says, her voice trembling, "but we burnt it."

In his frustration, Remos stalks up and down the room. He pauses to look again at Father, who stands there refusing to meet Remos's probing stare. In his work Remos surely has learned to read the expressions of people under stress, to tell when they are lying. He believes Father has the envelope.

I don't know what to do. If it is true that Father has the information against General López it might save our lives, but once he has the envelope, would Remos destroy our family? Our deaths would mean nothing to him.

To Father, Remos says, "I can tear your house apart. I can take your son and daughter back to prison, and you and your wife as well. Your son will tell you we have ways there of being persuasive, but all that takes time, and I am a man in a hurry." Remos releases the safety catch from his gun and points it at Mother. I think I will never breathe again. "Tell me where it is," he says to Father, "or I will kill her."

Silvia, we are helpless. If we move he might shoot. He is a desperate man. We stand there shaking. But Father is a doctor and is also good at searching the expression of a man for the truth. He sees Remos means what he says. At once he goes to a cushion and with trembling fingers opens the blade of a pocketknife. Even in this he is a careful surgeon as he cuts open the cushion. The stuffing oozes out. He reaches inside and draws out an envelope. Then he hands it to Remos.

With the gun in one hand Remos thumbs through the papers. A contented smile crosses his face. He says, "I am astounded at how much General López's wife must hate her husband to place this evidence in the hands of his enemies. There is enough here to crush him beneath my boot like the *cucaracha* he is."

Remos puts his gun back in its holster. He looks at us with a mild curiosity, as if he were leafing through a book and we caught his eye. "I could kill the four of you. No one would question me, but I have had enough of doing General López's dirty work. How furious he will be when he sees you have escaped, and how pleased his fury will make me." Remos reaches for the phone. We hear him give orders for four passports in our names. He says he must have four tickets to Madrid. Silvia, he has what he wants.

Remos is sending us to Spain.

Seville, Spain
1978

Silvia

IS it possible, Eduardo, that a year has gone by since we left Argentina? It is hard to believe we are safe here in Spain. Our city of Seville is one of Spain's oldest cities.

And we are not the first foreigners to escape to Seville! Romans, Visigoths, Muslims, Jews, and Christians have all had a hand in the city's history. The university we attend was built over four thousand years ago. There is so much history here we could drown in it.

Though you are with me every day I still write my letters to you with my secret thoughts, thoughts I cannot put into words. I don't speak of it to you, but in the dark my nightmares come back. Over and over I see myself dragged from our home and thrown into a car. I feel the cold dampness of the cell and hear the voice of Remos. Then I awake to daylight and safety.

You and I are always suspicious, so afraid that our new lives are just a dream that will end. So we seldom talk of what happened; instead we speak of Argentina, but not the Argentina that keeps us awake in the night. We are seldom far from one another. When we walk, we walk arm in arm. Last week for the first time we drew close to speaking of our haunting memories. We were sitting in my favorite place, the María Louisa Park, breathing in the fragrance of the orange blossoms, surrounded by fountains and flower gardens. I was sipping a *limonada*. You had your nose buried in a newspaper. From behind the newspaper I heard grumblings. I asked, "What's the matter?"

You complained, "The one time Argentina gets to host the World Cup soccer matches I'm stuck here in Spain."

I smiled. "I suppose you are happy that all the countries finally agreed to play in Argentina." At first several countries had refused to take part in the matches because of General Videla and his prisons, but now all the countries are there.

You said, "If the teams had refused to come to Argentina, it would have made the world see what

Videla was doing to the country. Still, with teams from all over the world and with hundreds of reporters at the games, some truths are sure to come out. I'd give anything to be there. I'd put on a demonstration they couldn't ignore."

I said, "In that case I'm glad you're here." Then I pointed out, "Netherlands's star player, Johan Cruijff, is refusing to play."

"I know. That's good for Argentina in two ways. First, everyone will hear what Cruijff has to say about our people in the prisons—and without Cruijff Argentina is more likely to beat Netherlands."

"Eduardo!" I said, pretending to be shocked. "That is so cynical. I wish none of the teams had agreed to go to Argentina. I don't care about the matches. I care about the prisoners. Think where *we* were a year ago."

You gave me a long look and I realized what a foolish thing I had said. "Did you think I would forget?" you whispered.

I reached for your hand. "I'm sorry. You were the one who truly suffered, I only complicated things."

"No. It was your information against López that saved us. Father says it destroyed López. Without that we would be in prison—or dead."

"If you had it to do over," I dared to ask, "would you?"

I saw you, Eduardo, struggling to give a dispassionate answer. I hear you often at night, moving about in your room, unable to sleep. You must have your nightmares just as I do. I think it unfair that we have nothing to say about what happens in our dreams.

Finally you told me, "I should have been more cautious. My ideals and my pride were all tangled. When I saw what was going on I felt a desperate need to change things. I didn't understand that to slay a dragon, you must creep up on it. I thought only of those the dragon was devouring. I gave no consideration to what my actions would mean for you and Mother and Father. I was a soldier marching into a battle with no plan."

On this first day of June, you and I and our parents and many of our exiled friends from Argentina are gathered around their television set. It is the opening day of the World Soccer match. We are not the only ones looking on. All the world is watching. The cameras focus on the stadium, and in a dramatic show, hundreds of white doves are released.

You are angry, Eduardo, and complain, "The dove is a sign of peace. There is no peace in Argentina."

The fans in the stadium scream with excitement. Suddenly the camera moves away from the soccer stadium. At the very moment when the generals want the world to see what a fine peaceful country Argentina is, the cameras show the Plaza de Mayo.

I reach for Mother's hand. "Look! They're showing the marching." The mothers are holding up signs for the camera: *Give Us Our Desaparecidos,* the signs say.

The cameras return to the match, but all the world has seen the mothers. People will ask questions. They will want answers. They will learn of the Disappeared.

Later that evening when the match is over and the guests have left, you and I, Eduardo, sit outside under the stars. I ask, "Eduardo, do you remember how Father would let us stay up until the sky was dark and he could point out the stars? Do you remember how we went with Father to the planetario and he told us the story of the Phoenix and how a small worm crawled from the nest the sun had destroyed? The sun warmed the little creature and turned it into a new and beautiful bird. Will that happen to Argentina?"

You shake your head. You will not say.

General Videla still rules Argentina, but it is said his days are numbered. You have had letters from

Montevideo. Teresa tells you she and her mother are safe. They hear nothing of Ramón. He is among the Desaparecidos, but still they hope. Isabela writes me that General López is ill and in prison. I try to feel some pity for him, but I have none. Señora López and Norberto, she says, are rumored to live together in a small apartment. I imagine them locked together for life, Norberto loathing his mother even more as his jailer.

When he is not at the hospital Father is also writing letters. His letters go to the editors of newspapers in countries around the world to protest General Videla's visits abroad. Father's letters follow Videla to Venezuela and the United States like diligent bloodhounds, urging those countries to pressure the general into freeing political prisoners.

Mother's furious poems about the families of the women she marched with have appeared like angry wasps in several Spanish publications. Eduardo, you are writing too. The articles of yours that you said Remos laughed at, as well as new articles you have written, are being secretly circulated in Buenos Aires among the students at the university. But I only listen and watch what is happening in Argentina. I am catching my breath. I am waiting for the nightmares to stop, then I will look around and see what is to be done.

The orange blossoms are in bloom all over the city. We breathe in their fragrance. We have a new life. Last week we went to see an American film, *Star Wars*. In the evenings we visit the cafés for tapas and dancing. You have a girlfriend with eyes like a doe to whom you are teaching the tango, but I suspect your thoughts are of Teresa. I am seeing a boy who is in my Spanish literature class. We study together in the library, our feet nudging one another under the table while we read *Don Quixote*.

Our new home is on the Guadalquivir River. Across the river is Triana, once a Gypsy settlement, shelter to another homeless people. On warm evenings when our windows are open we hear the flamenco music from the riverside cafés. I write back to Isabela and you, Eduardo, write back to Teresa. We write warm, friendly letters with no politics to excite the censors. In our letters we promise we will return to Argentina. Every morning we wait a little nervously for the other to come downstairs. Then we go on with our lives.

Epilogue

DURING the early seventies, Argentina, like so many countries—including our own—was experiencing a period of unrest. In the previous forty-six years, the country had twenty-one different administrations, some elected, some military juntas. The most colorful president during those years was General Juan Domingo Perón, a strong leader who with the support of his colorful second wife, Evita, granted women the right to vote and gained the support of working people.

Although Perón was democratically elected in 1946, many of his policies were those of a dictator. The military forced Perón to resign in 1955 and he was exiled to Spain. In 1973 Perón was returned to power. A year later he died, and his third wife, Isabel, succeeded him as president of Argentina.

Isabel was ineffectual in putting down the growing

rash of terrorism and revolution that was spreading throughout the country, led by two guerrilla forces, the PRT-ERP and the Montoneros. In 1973 alone there was an average of one terrorist attack a day, including bombings, kidnappings and assassinations, and attacks on police and military posts, nearly half of which took place in Buenos Aires.

In 1976 Isabel was defeated and General Jorge Rafael Videla, commander in chief of the armed forces, became president of Argentina, promising to bring order to the country. Argentina was eager for peace. At first General Videla was welcomed, but as arrests, often with no charges, became more frequent, as people were dragged from their homes in the dead of night and carried off to secret prisons and tortured, the people of Argentina turned against Videla and the military. The mothers began to march, demanding the return of their Disappeared, but to this day many have never been found.

In 1981 the presidency was transferred to General Roberto Viola, who began to work for a return from military to civilian rule. This alarmed the military, who forced General Viola out in 1982 and installed General Leopoldo Galtieri. When General Galtieri initiated a war with Great Britain over the Falkland Islands and then lost the war, the country rose up against the military and in 1983 elected a civilian, Raúl Alfonsín.

General López is an imaginary character, but General Videla is very real. In November of 1984 the National Commission Concerning the Disappearance of Persons published a report entitled *"Nunca Más,"* Never Again. Following the report the senior commanders who headed the government and the military during the years of the Desaparecidos were put on trial. One by one, 832 victims told their stories of kidnapping, torture, and execution. General Videla and Admiral Emilio Massero were sentenced to life in prison. Other members of the military received lesser penalties.

In October of 1989 President Carlos Menem issued a pardon to 277 officers who had been convicted of human rights violations. General Videla was not among those who received pardons, but in February of 1990 General Videla and the remaining prisoners were released. However, in June of 1997 General Videla was rearrested. After two months in prison he was allowed to return home, where he remains under house arrest. On September 6, 2006, a judge ruled that President Menem's pardons were unconstitutional, making possible a future re-trial of General Videla.

Argentina has not forgotten its *Desaparecidos*.

For Further Reading

Lewis, Daniel K. *The History of Argentina*. New York: Palgrave MacMillian, 2003.

Lewis, Paul H. *Guerrillas and Generals: The "Dirty War" in Argentina*. Westport, CT, and London: Praeger, 2001.

Mellibovsky, Matilde. *Circle of Love Over Death: Testimonies of the Mothers of the Plaza de Mayo*. Willimantic, CT: Curbstone Press, 1997.

Nouzeilles, Gabriela and Graciela Montaldo, eds. *The Argentina Reader: History, Culture, Politics*. Durham and London: Duke University Press, 2002.